# CHAPTER ONE

"Report?" Nathan asked as he entered the bridge from his ready room. He was feeling a bit anxious despite the fact that he was pretty sure what to expect. The hours had been long over the last few days, but they had still been a welcomed break from the chaos that had preceded them.

"Short-range just picked up a contact," Jessica reported. "He's still a ways out, but he's headed straight for us, and fast."

"Is it our guest?" The question was directed at Jalea, who had just stepped onto the bridge and came to stand beside Nathan and Jessica. She looked at the tactical display in front of Jessica, trying to determine the identity of the ship. She was still unfamiliar with the way the Aurora's systems displayed information.

"It is most likely him," Jalea told them, "but I cannot be sure without making voice contact."

"Suggest we go to battle stations, sir," Jessica urged. "With our limited crew and weapons, better safe than sorry."

"Agreed."

"Captain," Jalea protested, "it is important that you take no actions that might provoke him. If he changes his mind about helping us, I cannot promise that anyone else will."

"He's still coming in awfully fast," Jessica warned.

Nathan could sense the tension in Jessica's voice. She was usually quite calm in such situations, and if there was a hint of concern, Nathan felt it best to follow her advice.

"Sound general quarters," he ordered, "but do *not* deploy the rail guns yet."

They weren't exactly the orders she had hoped for, but Jessica understood his reasons. The incoming vessel was relatively small and, as of yet, had shown no signs of aggression other than its rapid approach.

"General quarters. No weapons deployment. Aye, sir." Jessica activated the ship-wide alert system. Status light panels located on overhead beams, above hatchways, and embedded in walls and bulkheads throughout the ship all suddenly changed from green to red, as the communications officer announced, "General quarters. General quarters. All hands assume combat stations."

"Time to intercept?" Nathan asked.

"One minute," Jessica answered. "He's still not slowing down."

"Is that him?" Cameron asked as she entered the bridge.

"We don't know yet," Nathan said.

"How can you not know?" Cameron wondered aloud as she took her station at the helm.

"All stations manned and ready," Jessica updated. "Thirty seconds to intercept."

All eyes were on the main view screen that wrapped around the front half of the bridge. The approaching ship started as nothing more than a tiny speck, hidden amongst all the other tiny specks against the starry background of space. It grew rapidly until its shape finally formed into something resembling a spacecraft, as it streaked past, barely missing them.

"Jesus!" Nathan exclaimed. The bridge was located deep within the ship, but every time something streaked past them in such a manner, it made him want to duck.

"He's coming back around," Jessica reported. "He's making another pass."

Jessica grimaced, clenching her teeth. Nathan could see that it was taking every ounce of willpower on her part to refrain from blasting the cocky little ship into a million pieces. "Steady, Ensign," Nathan mumbled as he leaned over the tactical console next to her, watching the display. Jessica just sneered at him.

"Message coming in," the communications officer announced.

"Put it on," Nathan ordered as he straightened back up.

*"Aurora, this is Tobin Marsh. I will land on your flight deck."* The signal immediately clicked off.

"Channel closed, sir," the comm officer reported.

"Arrogant little shit, isn't he?" Jessica muttered. After spending the last two years amongst the testosterone-filled Special Operations cadre, she had yet to become accustomed to the more well-mannered atmosphere of the bridge.

"He merely seeks to establish a position of strength before sitting down to negotiate the terms of his assistance," Jalea explained. "It is to be expected."

"He's coming around again, more slowly this time," Jessica reported. "Looks like he's doing just what he said. He's going to land."

"Get down there and meet him, Jess," Nathan ordered. "Then bring him to the briefing room."

"Yes, sir," she acknowledged as she departed.

Nathan turned to Jalea. "You're sure about this guy?"

"As I said before, this is not the first time we have utilized his services."

"Well he sure likes to make an entrance," Cameron added.

* * *

Jessica came to the bottom of the ramp to find her partner from Special Operations, Enrique Mendez, waiting for her. He carried a standard issue, close-quarters automatic weapon slung over his shoulder and a handgun holstered on his belt.

"Miss me?" Enrique held out a weapon for Jessica, smiling at her as she approached. It was the standard *Mister Charming* smile that he always tried on the ladies. She had always told him that it didn't work, but he never listened.

"Medical already cleared you for duty?" She looked at his hip, noticing the abnormal bulge from the bandage under his trousers.

"I didn't ask," he admitted. Jessica shot him a disapproving glance as she took the weapon from him. "Hey, I'm good to go, baby."

"Is that right?" As she passed by, Jessica patted the bulge on his thigh where he had been wounded a few days ago, causing him to wince slightly.

"Damn, Jess. Play nice, now," he scolded as he fell in behind her.

They continued down the corridor, entering the main hatch to the hangar bay. Inside there were two marines, Sergeants Weatherly and Holmes. Thus far, other than Enrique, Weatherly and Holmes were the only other people on board that she was sure could shoot straight.

"Should only be one guy on this thing," she announced as she entered. "But he appears to be a bit on the arrogant side. Either way, let's play it safe. Got it?"

"Yes, sir," they both agreed.

"Enrique, you and Holmes take starboard. We'll go port side. Forty-five degree attack angles. If it gets ugly, try to maim, not kill." She didn't wait for a response. Instead, she immediately trotted off to her right and made her way down the sides of the hangar bay until she reached a good position behind some large containers on the port side of the bay, facing aft. Across the bay from her, Enrique and Holmes were taking up similar positions.

"We're in position," she announced to the bridge over her comm-set.

"*Copy. The airlock is nearly cycled. The doors should be opening momentarily,*" Nathan reported over the comms.

A few moments later, the massive door on the center transfer airlock began sliding up into the ceiling, accompanied by the sound of the gears and motors driving it. Beyond the door was the same spacecraft that only minutes ago had been buzzing about their ship like an annoying insect. They watched as the ship began to slowly roll forward from the transfer airlock into the hangar bay. Once clear of the airlock, the door automatically closed again, ready for another recovery. Even though they had left Earth without any of their auxiliary spacecraft, the airlocks were automated so as to enable the launch and recovery of spacecraft even during complete control failures.

Unlike the time she had lain in wait for the arrival of Marak's ship a few days ago, this time the hangar was fully lit, and she made no attempt to conceal her position from their guest. As a counter to his arrogance, she wished him to be fully aware that his presence did not intimidate them. It was simply another angle of the psychological side of warfare that she had been taught in spec-ops.

The small ship rolled to a stop, its engines winding down as its systems vented unknown vapors. The ship had a long, cylindrical fuselage resembling a flattened cigar, with short stubby wings and a pair of tail-mounted engines. She had numerous maneuvering ports located all about her fuselage, but from what Jessica could see, the ship was unarmed.

A small boarding hatch about a meter aft of the cockpit windows suddenly swung downward, becoming a boarding ramp complete with small steps that folded out automatically as the hatch fully deployed. A slender man in his mid-thirties, with jet black hair and a melodramatic goatee, stepped out through the hatch and looked about. He immediately saw the four weapons pointed at him from either side of the bay and assumed a submissive posture, his hands forward and held up, for all to observe their emptiness. "I carry no arms," he announced. "I pose no threat to you."

"Keep your hands up where I can see them and we'll have no problems," Jessica instructed confidently.

The man looked at her for a moment, finally deciding that she was not the type that would have a problem pulling the trigger if necessary. "As you wish," he agreed, holding his hands up even higher and farther away from his body as he continued down the step ladder. "Please do not harm me. I am here at the request of Jalea Torren. She is with you; is she not?"

"She is," Jessica replied. The man continued toward her. "That's far enough," she added with more urgency. "Hands up on your head, please. Stay perfectly still and everything will be fine." Jessica rose from her cover and headed toward him, gesturing to Enrique to do the same. Weatherly and Holmes both stayed back, ready to cover the two ensigns should things turn bad.

Suddenly, the hatch to the man's ship closed of its own accord, causing Jessica to stop in her tracks. "I told you not to move!" she warned.

"I did not. I assure you!" the man assured her. "It was automatic."

"Is anything else going to move... automatically?" she asked, her weapon trained on his face.

"No, nothing. My ship was only securing itself."

"Search him."

Enrique approached cautiously and began patting him down, searching for hidden weapons.

The man looked surprised by the pat-down. "I assure you I am unarmed, as promised."

"A girl can never be too careful," she mused. The man returned her smile, recognizing her sarcasm.

"Indeed," he answered. "I suppose you will now take me to see your captain?"

"Right this way," Jessica instructed, gesturing for him to follow her partner.

* * *

Tobin Marsh strode confidently into the briefing

room. Upon spotting Jalea, he extended his arms, taking her by the shoulders and giving her a polite kiss on each cheek as he spoke words that, in their language, were surely a charming and polite greeting. Their initial pleasantries concluded, she turned to face Nathan and Cameron. Both were standing on the opposite side of the table from them.

"Tobin Marsh," Jalea began in English, "may I introduce Captain Nathan Scott and Commander Cameron Taylor of the Aurora."

"It is my distinct pleasure to meet you both," Tobin greeted in proper, although considerably accented, English. His accent, although similar to Jalea's, was somehow different. There was something a little less proper about his syntax, despite the fact that he was obviously trying very hard to speak perfect *Angla*, as they called it. "I trust my unorthodox arrival did not give you too much cause for alarm," he added, casting a sidelong glance at Jessica, who stood against the wall on the same side of the table as Nathan and Cameron. Tobin reached out his hand in greeting, shaking first Cameron's and then Nathan's.

"Yes, your style seemed a bit aggressive," Nathan admitted politely, "but as we are new to this region of space, we tried not to attach undue significance."

"You are? Of this I was not aware." Tobin's curiosity was evident. "From what region do you hail?"

Nathan could see the look of warning coming from Jessica's eyes as he spoke. "Let's just say, *for now*, that we come from quite far away."

"Really? Now you do have my interest, Captain. Is your origin really such a secret?"

"We've only just met, sir. For the time being,

where we are *from* is not related to the services we seek. Unless, of course, knowledge of our origin is a condition of your service. If this *is* the case, we will not waste any more of your time." Nathan was surprised at how easily both the statement and the appropriate body language he used to indicate his intent to depart the room had come to him. After all those years of watching his father in the political arena, apparently some of those skills had rubbed off on him.

"It is not a condition, Captain," Tobin explained. He too was comfortable at such negotiations, showing no undue reaction to Nathan's statements or posturing. "It was merely a curiosity, for which I apologize." Tobin bowed his head in a polite gesture of concession to Nathan, indicating that he would yield to Nathan's requirement for secrecy as to their point of origin. "Now, tell me, Captain, what services might you seek?"

"These people are in need of many things," Jalea began, "primarily a place of refuge where they might make repairs to their ship, as well as the procurement of food, and perhaps some supplies." Jalea gave Tobin a stern look with her next statement. "And these services should be... discreet."

"Yes, yes, as you said in your original message. These things are not difficult to provide," Tobin assured them, "especially in the Haven system. Discretion is *why* people come here, after all. However, as providing such services could put me at considerable risk, I would need to know exactly whose attention you wish to avoid." Tobin smiled, knowing that on this point he could stand firm.

"We have had some unexpected, and unprovoked I might add, trouble... with a certain government,"

Nathan explained.

"Yes. I observed the damage to your ship as I approached. It was quite a bit of trouble, it appears. I assume this government is the same one our friend Jalea here also does not have good relations with?"

Nathan found it amusing, in a disgusting sort of way, that even on the other side of the galaxy, negotiations were still the same. "That would be a safe assumption."

"I see." Tobin stroked his goatee as he pretended to consider the request. Nathan knew full well that he would provide the services they were requesting. Tobin would not have flown for more than a day in a small ship had he not intended to conduct business with them.

"Then, you can provide these services?"

"Yes, Captain. I believe we can come to an agreement."

"And what compensation do you require?" Nathan did not want to be surprised later.

"Please, Captain. I am only here because I have a life debt to not only Jalea, but many of her people as well."

"No offense intended, Tobin, but surely, there must be a way for you to receive some sort of compensation. It seems only fair since your debt is not owed to us."

"You understand me only too well, Captain. I can see that you are a man wiser than your years." Tobin smiled again. Nathan decided not to speak further, waiting instead for the other shoe to fall. "You are correct. There *is* a way in which we can all come out ahead in this... *situation.* Tell me, Captain. How much has Jalea told you about Haven?"

"I'm afraid there has been little discussion about

this system. We've been a bit busy the last few days. Perhaps you'd care to enlighten us?"

"Surely." Tobin leaned back in his chair before beginning. "Haven is a refuge of sorts. It is a place where people, and ships, that seek safe and discreet harbor may come. It is also a center for unregistered *trading,* if you will, in various *commodities.*"

Nathan leaned toward Cameron as Tobin continued to describe his world. "Must be the space pirates you spoke of," he jeered under his breath. Cameron rolled her eyes as Nathan turned his attention back to Tobin, who had not even noticed his sidebar.

"And it's possible for us to hide there, even with so many ships in the area?"

"Haven's primary business is the harvesting of her vast ring systems. There is only one planet in the Haven system, a gas giant with many moons. Haven City, and the only spaceport in the system, is on one of those moons. The planet's rings are full of all manner of ores, minerals, and water ice. And the planet's atmosphere is rich in many useful gases as well. Ships come from all over the quadrant to fill their holds with the resources harvested here, for which they pay a duty to the powers that control this system."

"So there's a government of sorts here?" Nathan was a bit concerned about the possible complications that might arise due to the presence of a local government.

"I wouldn't call them a *government*, Captain. It's more of a *family business,* so to speak. However, I would advise you to treat them with much the same respect that you might give to any *legitimate* government, if you understand my meaning."

"Of course."

"As far as hiding your ship, it is simply a matter of getting you authorization to harvest the rings like any other ship. As long as you have a proper transponder that identifies your ship, no one will give you a second look; I assure you. And there are so many ships traveling in and out of the rings on a daily basis that anything you do, short of armed combat, *will* go unnoticed."

"And how does this arrangement benefit you?"

"Ah, yes." This brought a sly grin to Tobin's face. "If you indeed intend to procure additional supplies from Haven City's *lucrative* markets, you will need something of value to exchange. No offense intended, Captain, but your ship does not appear to be one that carries great wealth. While you are posing as a harvesting vessel, I will provide you with a harvesting team from Haven. They can use your ship as a staging platform from which to conduct harvesting operations. Some of the harvested materials can be used to purchase the supplies that you need, and some can be kept by you for your own purposes. And of course, some will be used to compensate the workers, as well as a modest fee for myself in exchange for acting as your intermediary."

"I see," Nathan responded. He looked at Cameron and Jalea. Neither of them offered any indication for or against Tobin's proposal. He was afraid to look at Jessica, as he knew how she would feel about bringing more strangers on board. "Well, it is a very interesting offer. I trust you will not be insulted if I ask for a few minutes to discuss it with my staff."

"Not at all, Captain. Not at all."

"Thank you." Nathan turned to Jalea. "Would you mind taking our guest for a stroll? We'll contact you when we're ready to speak further."

"As you wish, Captain." Jalea rose from the table and headed for the exit.

"I will await your decision, Captain," Tobin announced as he stood.

"I'll try not to keep you waiting." Nathan offered a sincere smile as Tobin and Jalea left the room, one of the marines following them out the door. Nathan held one hand up, indicating for Jessica and Cameron to wait until after the door closed before speaking.

"Okay, let's hear it," Nathan said after the door closed.

"I don't trust either one of them," Cameron stated.

"Well that goes without saying," Nathan agreed, leaning back in his chair, "but we have to do something. We can't just sit out here in the middle of nowhere."

"Why not?" Cameron asked. "Not forever, of course. But why *can't* we just sit out here and fix everything we can before we move on? It's safer than flying into that system full of who-knows-what."

"What are we going to do for food, Cam? We're down to nuts and dried fruit. And we'll be out of that in another day or two."

"I don't know, Nathan. Maybe there's something we can trade for some food. Maybe have this Tobin character ferry something out to us."

"I don't think that's what he has in mind. He's obviously angling for a larger score here."

"Yeah, that's what I'm afraid of," Cameron insisted.

Nathan turned to look at Jessica. "Well, you're awfully quiet. Surely you've got something to say about all this."

Jessica, who had been leaning against the wall the entire time, stepped over to the table and sat on the edge, turning to face the two of them. "Look, the whole setup stinks; there's no doubt about it. But I don't see as we have much choice. We need food. We need supplies. But more importantly, we need *intelligence*, and a hell of a lot more of it than Jalea is willing to dole out. We're not gonna jump or blast our way back to Earth. We have to think our way home. And to do that, we need to know exactly what we're up against. That means we *can't* just hide out here in the void. We have to bump elbows with the locals. We have to interact. That's the only way to gather reliable intel."

Nathan looked at Cameron. "She's right, you know."

"Yeah, I know." Cameron was obviously frustrated. The situation they were about to fly into was full of unknowns, which was something Cameron did not care for. "I just wish we knew more beforehand."

"I think that's the point she's trying to make." Nathan turned back to Jessica. "So what do you propose?"

"We need boots on the ground. Our own eyes and ears soaking up as much intel as possible."

"Are you proposing you go down to the surface?"

"I'm proposing *we* go down there, along with some backup, of course."

"Me? Why me?" Nathan was a bit shocked that she had suggested he go with her.

"Well, you seem to have a knack with negotiations. You're good with people. But you're not that observant of what's going on around you."

"I'll try to work on that," he promised.

"That's where I come in."

"You're assuming he has room for all of you in that little ship of his," Cameron pointed out.

"Well if he doesn't, I'm sure he can find one that does," Jessica said. "It doesn't sound like we're gonna be too far away from this Haven place."

"Then we're agreed," Nathan said, looking at each of them. It was obvious that Jessica was in agreement. It was equally obvious that Cameron was not.

"Sorry, Cam. Two against one; you lose." He smiled. "Call them back in," he said to Jessica.

"This isn't a democracy," Cameron reminded him, a scowl on her face. "You're the captain. You don't *ask* for a vote."

"Hey, gimme a break. I'm new at this, remember?"

Moments later, Tobin and Jalea returned to the briefing room, their escort in tow. After routine pleasantries were exchanged, Nathan spoke. "We've decided to accept your offer, Mister Marsh. But there are a few conditions." Tobin gave no indication that he intended to speak, so Nathan continued. "First, all personnel that you provide shall be restricted to the hangar deck, without exception. Anyone caught off the hangar deck will be forcibly detained, at a minimum. Second, all activity on the hangar deck will be closely monitored by armed personnel who will have standing orders to use deadly force if necessary." A stern look came over Nathan's face. "In this there can be no negotiation. We are in unknown space. By your own description, Haven is not exactly a safe place, especially for strangers such as ourselves. I trust these conditions will be acceptable."

"Of course, Captain. I understand your

need to maintain the security of your vessel, especially considering your recent governmental entanglements," he put delicately.

"And lastly, if there is room in your vessel, a few of us would like to accompany you to the surface to take a look around, so to speak."

This did cause a reaction from Tobin. "Captain, you yourself just acknowledged that Haven is not the safest of worlds, especially for strangers. Going there does not seem worth the risk at this point. Haven can be a *very* dangerous place."

"I suspect we'll be able to handle ourselves should something unexpected occur. But I appreciate your concern."

Tobin could see that Nathan was adamant in his desire to visit the surface of Haven and decided it was best not to press him on the issue. "As you wish, Captain. I can accommodate up to six passengers in my ship. However, due to the space restrictions, I would suggest waiting until you are in position within the rings of Haven before transferring to the surface."

"Of course," Nathan agreed. "And as for your compensation, we are only interested in whatever portion of the harvested resources is required to pay for what supplies we are able to procure while on Haven. Anything else you and your people are able to haul away you are welcome to divide however you wish."

Tobin's eyes widened slightly at Nathan's surprising offer. "That is very generous of you, Captain. Might I inquire as to how long you intend to remain in our system?"

"Only as long as is necessary to obtain the supplies we seek. To remain longer would be...

unwise." Nathan smiled.

"Very well then, Captain. It appears we have an arrangement," he stated, standing and offering his hand to seal the deal.

"It appears so," Nathan agreed, shaking Tobin's hand.

"Might I inquire as to how long it will take your ship to reach Haven?"

Nathan turned to look at Cameron. "About seven hours," she told them.

"I understand that you have a transponder for us to use."

"Yes. Once installed, it will identify you as a Volonese cargo ship," Tobin explained. "They are varied and not uncommon in this region of space. Even if inspected visually, it is doubtful anyone would become suspicious. And if they did, Volon is sufficiently distant. Verification of your identity would take far longer than your planned stay in our system."

"And how long will it take to install this device?"

"Less than an hour, I would expect. I will require the assistance of one of your technicians."

"I'll see to it," he assured Tobin. "Jalea, would you please take Mister Marsh to engineering. I will contact the chief engineer and let him know you're coming."

Jalea nodded, rose, and led Tobin out of the room, again with their armed escort trailing them. Once they had left the room, Nathan turned to Jessica.

"You don't have to say it," she said before he could speak. "I'll make sure they're both under constant scrutiny," she promised on her way out.

"Thanks." Nathan turned to Cameron. The look on her face told of her disapproval of his plan. "I know, Cam. I'm not crazy about it either. Just tell Abby to always have an escape jump plotted and ready, just in case."

"You bet," she agreed as she rose to exit.

"We'll get underway just as soon as that transponder is installed and working."

"Yes, sir," she halfheartedly agreed as she headed out of the briefing room. "I just hope you know what you're doing."

"So do I," he admitted. Nathan leaned back in his chair and let out a long, slow breath. His mind was racing at the thought of what lie ahead. Only days ago, they had left Earth on what they thought was a routine training cruise. After an unexpected string of events, they were now stranded a thousand light years from home in a busted-up ship with only a fraction of their crew. They were almost out of food, and they still had no idea how they were going to get home. At least now, however, they might not starve to death.

\* \* \*

"Perhaps the code you entered is not working." Vladimir was frustrated. They had been attempting to get the transponder provided by Tobin to work with the Aurora's navigational beacon for over an hour, and he was beginning to lose his patience with the alien technology.

"It will work," Tobin insisted. "It will just take time. Your ship is still well outside the system. At this distance, it will take several hours for the signal to reach Haven, and then for the confirmation signal to travel back out to us."

"And why do we need this device?"

"All ships entering the system must register with the system controllers. This requires you to spend several hours in port undergoing thorough inspections, creating trader accounts. It is all very involved and would not serve your need for discretion. This device will identify your ship as belonging to a small company that occasionally comes to harvest the rings. When they receive the signal from this transponder, the controllers will simply log you into their tracking system, tallying up charges as you conduct business within the system. No one will ever give you a second glance."

"Charges? We have to pay charges? What happens if we cannot pay?" Vladimir wondered. He was pretty sure there were no funds to speak of on board the Aurora.

"That would not be wise," Tobin warned. "The family that currently controls Haven is not known for their forgiveness."

"How did you get this device?"

"Anyone can *purchase* a transponder," Tobin explained. "It is the *codes* that are difficult to acquire without going through the registration process. Luckily, I know the right people in the right places." Tobin smiled.

"It is that easy?" Vladimir wasn't sure he believed everything the stranger was telling him.

"I did not say it was easy," Tobin corrected, "but Haven offers many things, *if* one knows where to look."

Vladimir also smiled, as he realized that no matter where you went, there was always a black market of some kind. Apparently it was no different in this part of the galaxy.

"I believe everything is in working order," Tobin

assured him as he punched in a code. Upon pressing the last key, the display on the device went blank for a moment, and then a single word appeared. It was in bold and flashed three times before becoming steady. But it was in Angla, which, although similar to English in its spoken form, used some odd variations in characters.

"What does that mean?" Vladimir asked.

"The device is now locked," Tobin announced nonchalantly.

"Locked? In what way?" Vladimir was not sure he liked the sound of that.

"Unless the code is locked, it will not appear to be valid to the controllers."

Vladimir still did not like the idea of anything being *locked*, but Tobin's explanation made sense. "How will we know it is safe to proceed?"

"When your ship approaches Haven, if you are not attacked, you will know."

Vladimir looked at Tobin, his eyes wide and his brow raised in doubt.

"Do not worry; it will be fine. I have done this many times," Tobin assured him.

"I'm sorry. I do not mean to doubt you. It just seems too easy."

"Yes, of course. But you must understand, the family does not really care if you *are* who you say you are. They only care that they get paid. As long as they receive their compensation, they will not question your identity." Tobin chuckled. "Corruption has its advantages." Tobin stood, satisfied that the installation had been completed. "You may tell your captain it is now safe to enter the system."

*"Bridge, engineering,"* Vladimir's voice called over the comm-system.

Nathan stood beside the communications officer, who was still using the port auxiliary station until the regular comm station at the rear of the bridge was repaired. He gestured to the comm officer to open the channel before he spoke. "Yeah, Vlad. Go ahead."

*"Nathan, the transponder is installed, and I am told it is working properly. Tobin says we can get underway whenever we are ready."*

"Very well. Bridge out." Nathan turned back toward Jessica, who was standing at the tactical station. "Any contacts in the area?"

"Not since Tobin arrived," she answered.

"Kaylah, is that thing transmitting?" Nathan asked Ensign Yosef, the science officer who had been manning the sensors for the last few days.

"Yes, sir, it is. Regular pulses, wide band, omni-directional. However, that signal will take several hours to reach Haven, sir."

"So we'll arrive shortly after the signal does?"

"Yes, sir, by a few hours, depending on our approach velocity."

Nathan turned to look at Jalea, who was standing at the rear of the bridge near the port entrance. "Can they see us out here?"

"I do not believe they regularly scan this far beyond their own borders. They would have no reason to do so. And even if they did, a single ship this far out would be difficult to spot, especially one that is not moving."

"Maybe we shouldn't look like we've just been sitting out here all this time," Jessica added. "It might look suspicious."

"Good thinking," Nathan commended. "Cameron, I assume you've already plotted a course into the system."

"Of course," she responded, "hours ago."

"Doctor Sorenson," Nathan turned to face her, "you have an escape jump plotted?"

"About a dozen variations, all along our proposed route into the system," she assured him.

"Very well." Nathan thought for a moment, hoping that they weren't about to make a mistake. "Let's get underway. Communications, alert all hands to prepare for acceleration."

"Aye, sir," the comm officer acknowledged.

"Helm, take us to Haven. Bring her up to maximum velocity as quickly as possible then start a gradual deceleration curve. I want us to look like we just dropped out of FTL on our way in."

"Aye, Captain. Bringing her up sharply to maximum sub-light velocity." As Cameron began entering commands at the helm station, the comm officer's voice could be heard in the background as he warned the crew to brace for sudden acceleration. The Aurora's inertial dampeners were still not fully repaired, and Nathan had to hold onto the tactical console to keep from falling over as the main engines were quickly brought up to maximum thrust levels. The ship lurched forward and began to accelerate quickly, forcing Nathan to shakily make his way to the command chair in order to avoid falling.

"How long will it take us to reach Haven?" he asked as he plopped down in his chair at the center of the bridge.

"About six hours." Due to their insufficient numbers, Cameron was forced to serve as both pilot and navigator, on top of her responsibilities as executive officer. Nathan had offered to handle the navigation for her, but unless the situation warranted otherwise, she felt better managing on her own. Although there was no denying Nathan's natural piloting abilities, she had never been impressed with his navigational skills.

After a short period of acceleration at full power, the ship reached her maximum sub-light speed. "Velocity at point seven five light," Cameron announced. "Mains are offline. Beginning deceleration burn."

Cameron brought the main engines offline and began a slow, steady deceleration burn using the forward braking thrusters. The burn would take nearly five hours to complete, bringing them down to just the right velocity and allowing them to be captured by the gravity well of the gas giant that Haven orbited. Compared to the main engines, the noise and sensation of the deceleration burn was almost nonexistent, making it easy for the crew to move about the ship without fear of losing their footing.

"Very well. Secure from acceleration stations."

"We are now entering the Haven system, Captain," Ensign Yosef announced.

"Let's hope that thing works," Nathan muttered.

\* \* \*

The medical section, although still full of patients, was at least clean and orderly once again. The chaos that had lasted more than twenty-four hours had finally subsided, and Doctor Chen and a handful of volunteers had managed to get a workable routine in place. She had expanded her facility by having the crew quarters nearest to medical evacuated in order to turn them into long-term care rooms, nearly tripling her capacity. But it was a challenge to routinely check on every patient under her care, even with the assistance of others as well as every piece of monitoring gear they could get their hands on. She had even taken some of the bio-monitors from EVA suits to monitor patients in nearby rooms.

Despite the young physician's best efforts, they had still lost another three members of their crew over the last two days. One of them had not been expected to survive his wounds. But the injuries of the other two had not been that severe. They had succumbed to infections due to the lack of medicine on board, something that never would have happened in a proper hospital.

Nathan had come by to check on Doctor Chen and her patients at least once per day, usually under the guise of having his own wound checked. But she knew better. He was coming to check on his crew. She knew that he still felt guilty for every one of their injuries, and even more so for the ones that had not survived. Admittedly, she had also blamed him at first, but as details of the chain of events that had befallen them became available, she realized that he had done the best he could under unbelievably difficult circumstances. She knew it had not been his fault, as did most of the crew. She also knew that he would continue to blame himself for some time to come.

She was not surprised when Nathan again walked into the main treatment area, stopping by each bed to spend a moment with the members of his crew. She expected that he didn't really have the spare time to spend visiting patients. Surely he had many other things to attend to that were of higher priority. But perhaps he needed these visits as much, if not more so, than her patients did.

She had seen this type of behavior before. During her internship back on Earth, she had spent time as a volunteer in a field hospital located near a border dispute between two warring tribal nations. Despite the global unity that had come about due to the discovery of the Data Ark, there had still been a few places on Earth where lands were controlled by the tribes that had lived on them for centuries. A group of about fifty soldiers had been overrun by the enemy, and the unit's commander had also spent considerable time in the treatment wards visiting his wounded soldiers. The look on his face had been similar to the one she now saw on Nathan's.

She waited at the far end of the room for him to make his rounds, using his visit as an excuse to take a break herself. She sat in the utility room on the far side of the treatment area, watching through the doorway. She had a stash of nuts and dried fruit on which to nibble from time to time. She hadn't sat down and eaten a proper meal in several days, and sleep had only come in short naps at best.

It took Nathan nearly half an hour to visit everyone in the treatment area. She had no idea if he ever managed to visit the others recuperating in nearby cabins. She simply assumed he had.

"How's the leg?" she asked as he entered the utility room.

"Pretty much healed, I expect," he bragged, bouncing slightly on it as if testing its sturdiness. "I'm not limping anymore, and it only throbs a bit from time to time."

"Yeah, it'll probably do that for a few more days.

It's a side effect of the bone-knitting serum. It'll pass."

"What about you? How are you holding up?"

"I've been better," she chuckled, "but I'm managing to snack here and there, and take quick naps. Eventually everyone will stabilize enough that I can get a bit more rest. Until then, I'll survive." She took a sip from a bottle of water before continuing. "So how's it going out there?"

"That's one of the things I wanted to talk to you about. We're headed for a world called Haven."

"That explains the acceleration. You might want to give us more than a few seconds warning next time. It takes us a few minutes to prepare for something like that down here," she scolded.

Nathan suddenly felt guilty. "Sorry about that. It never occurred to me," he admitted.

"So why are we going to this place, anyway?"

"We're using a local contact of Jalea's to try and get some food and supplies. I was wondering if there was anything in particular you might need."

"Another doctor would be nice," she said, only half joking.

"From the sounds of this place, I doubt that's possible."

Doctor Chen shrugged. "Real food would be nice. I'd ask for medicine and such, but I don't like the idea of using strange substances on my patients. I've got enough trouble as it is."

"Food is at the top of the list," he told her, "and as much as we can get of it."

"By the way," she added, "make sure anyone who goes down to the surface comes by for medical screenings when they get back. We don't want to bring any strange diseases on board."

The idea had also never occurred to Nathan, just like a lot of things recently. Every time one of them came up, it served to remind him how unqualified he was to be in command. "Yeah, Doc, I'll make sure we do that."

* * *

Despite the fact that they had no prepared meals left to eat, Nathan and Vladimir still managed to meet for lunch each day. It was an excuse to take a break from their seemingly endless duties, and it provided Nathan with a way to keep up on the status of repairs without having to constantly nag Vladimir for progress reports. Although he was a gifted engineer and systems technician, getting him to write even the shortest of reports was like pulling teeth. Considering all there was to do just to keep the ship running—let alone trying to repair her—it was understandable.

Until this morning, they had been down to nuts and dried fruit in the pantry, and even that had needed to be rationed. Cameron, who was turning out to be quite a resourceful executive officer, had realized that all the escape pods were fully loaded with dehydrated meal kits. They weren't the tastiest things around, but all you needed was a cup of hot water and you had a filling meal. Since they had at least fifty escape pods and only a skeleton crew, it would buy them some time. Nathan didn't want to use all of the escape pod rations for fear that they might someday need to use the pods for their intended purpose. So they had used EVA suits to access the escape pods in the forward section of the ship, which was still open to the vacuum of space.

Until that portion of the ship was repaired, no one would be using those escape pods.

"What's on the menu today?" Nathan picked up the meal pouch that Vladimir had dropped on the table in front of him, giving it a look. It didn't appear terribly appetizing.

"Something with noodles," Vladimir said, "but is supposed to have meat in it," he added as he set the small pot of boiling hot water on the table between them. Nathan peeled back the cover on the container and poured in some of the hot water.

"Anything is better than nuts and dried fruit," Nathan insisted as he stirred the contents to thoroughly distribute the hot water.

"We hope. But it cannot be as bad as meal replacement bar," Vladimir added as he stirred his meal.

"So, how go the repairs?" It was the first question that Nathan always asked, as it usually took Vladimir most of their brief meal period to explain everything he and his staff were doing.

"It is going. Everything that can be fixed is being fixed. But for many systems we will need to manufacture new components in order to repair them. We have several component printers and even some machining equipment stored in the hangar bay, but they have not yet been installed. But, we have propulsion and maneuvering, and we have most of the rail guns working. Even some of the ones that were not yet connected—they are also working—thanks to Danik and Allet."

"Who?"

"The two rebel engineers," Vladimir explained. "How do you call them, *Karuzari*? They are very good. They are working in the torpedo room now.

They will have the port auto-loaders ready soon. Maybe even the aft loaders as well. The starboards tubes, however, they are badly damaged and will not be available for some time."

"Oh, I was wrong," Nathan said, his face souring as he took his first taste of his reconstituted meal. His face took on a sour expression. "Fruit and nuts are better."

"Hey, at least it has meat in it," Vladimir exclaimed as he began to shovel the reconstituted mixture into his mouth, "although I am not sure what kind."

"So these guys are that good, huh?"

"Oh yes! They even improved power transfer to the rail guns, increasing their rate of fire by ten percent. They could boost it more, but there are other priorities." Vladimir stopped shoveling food into his mouth for a moment, adding, "You know, our systems appear to be very simple to them."

"Damn, this really is bad," Nathan stated, not sure he could finish his meal kit.

"Stop whining. It is food. Listen, Nathan, you are going down to the surface of Haven, yes?"

"Yeah, that's the plan."

"What is it you are going to do there?"

"Try to get some food and supplies, and some intel if possible. Why?"

"I think I should go down there as well."

"Why?"

"According to Tobin, there is a vigorous black market there. Perhaps I can find some interesting technology, maybe something that would be of use to us."

"You think that's possible?" The idea had not occurred to Nathan.

"I think it is worth a look. We could use many

things right now."

"Aren't you busy here?"

"Most important things are working," he insisted, "and my people will continue working in my absence."

"Yeah, okay. I don't see why not."

"I would like to bring Danik and Allet as well. They would be helpful in locating useful technology. Besides, it was Danik's idea," Vladimir admitted.

"Well, I'm not sure we can bring them both. There's only room for six passengers on Tobin's shuttle. And Jessica wants to take some muscle along. But I agree it would be a good idea. Maybe you can just bring one of them."

"You were right, Nathan," Vladimir admitted.

"About only bringing one of them?"

"No, this stuff is bad. Very bad."

* * *

"Have you been sleeping in here?" Jessica asked, noticing the pillow and blanket on the couch as she followed Nathan into the captain's ready room. "You have quarters, you know."

"They're all the way down on C deck. It's easier to just take naps here," he explained.

"No, I meant the captain's quarters. They're right down the hall."

Nathan shook his head, his expression changing to one of trepidation. "No, too soon," he protested, waving his hands slightly.

"Wuss," she muttered as she plopped down on the couch. Just like everyone else on board, she had gotten very little sleep over the last few days.

"That's *Captain Wuss* to you, Ensign."

"Yeah, I was gonna ask you about that. Don't

you think your *Chief of Security* should at least be a lieutenant?"

"Why? You looking to be next in line for command if Cam and I get killed?"

"Hell no! Just looking for a raise in pay."

"Let's wait and see how long you keep the job."

"What's that supposed to mean?!"

"What's what supposed to mean?" Cameron asked as she entered.

"Nothing. How far out are we?" Nathan asked.

"A couple hours."

"You guys get a chance to take a break and eat something?" Nathan looked at them both, seeing that neither of them indicated they had so much as left the bridge since their last meeting several hours ago.

"Well, see to it that you at least get some food into you," he insisted. "Both of you. And stay away from the noodle and meat thingy. Trust me on this," he added as he sat down behind his desk. "So, have we given any thought as to what we're going to be shopping for on Haven?"

"Well, food is the number one priority," Cameron began. "And one of the environmental systems techs suggested that we look for some seasonings and spices as well. He used to be a chef before he joined the fleet. Makes sense that if we're going to start cooking local food, we might want some local spices to go with it."

"Yeah. Doctor Chen pointed out to me earlier that we are setting foot on an alien world with a race of people that, although human, could carry many diseases that our immune systems aren't ready for. She suggested we take caution while on the surface. She also wants everyone who goes to the surface to report for a full medical screening when we get back. So I was thinking, we probably should go over any consumables we bring on board before we start eating them."

"Agreed," Cameron said.

"She also gave me a list of possible pharmaceutical substitutes to be on the lookout for as well," Nathan continued, "antibiotics, pain killers, basic stuff like that. They were stocked up to normal peacetime levels when we left. But with all the wounded, she's already running out of the basics. Two people died because of a lack of antibiotics."

"You really think we'll find something out here that's safe for us to use?" Cameron wondered.

"Well, they're humans, just like us, so it stands to reason that they'd have similar meds and such. And since we're already seeing evidence of superior technology in some areas, maybe they have better medicines as well."

"One can only hope," Jessica added.

"I don't know," Cameron objected. "It sounds kind of risky to me."

"She's not too keen on the idea either. In fact, I pretty much had to talk her into it. But we don't know how long we're going to be out here or how often we're going to have an opportunity like this."

"Anything else?" Cameron asked, taking notes on her data pad.

"Yeah, Vladimir wants to go down and check out the local black market for useful technologies."

Jessica had not been paying close attention to the conversation until Nathan mentioned the black market. "Whoa, that might not be such a hot idea," she warned. "Black markets tend to be fairly dangerous places to hang out. At least on Earth they are. Vlad doesn't seem like the right personality type to work the black market—too friendly and outspoken, you know?"

"He wanted to bring the rebel engineers with him as guides. He seems to have a lot of confidence in them."

"I don't know about that either," Jessica warned. "I haven't really dealt with them all that much. If they're anything like their lady friend, I wouldn't trust them any farther than I can throw them."

"Maybe you're right," Nathan admitted, "but the more I think about it, the more I think that Vlad is right. With their understanding of both the local technology and our own, they would be invaluable down there. Maybe it's worth the risk."

"Is there even room?" Cameron asked.

"Well, there's only room for six passengers, according to Tobin. So maybe we leave some muscle behind?"

"No way," Jessica insisted. "I'd rather take the muscle than some shifty rebel."

Nathan was a little surprised by her characterization of the rebels, but he understood her point. He had selected her as his interim security chief because of her training in such matters, so he felt it best to heed her advice. "Very well, you keep your two guys. I'll have Vladimir bring only one of the rebels with us."

The comm-system buzzer sounded. *"Captain, bridge,"* the communications officer called.

Nathan stabbed at the comm with his finger. "Go ahead."

*"Captain, communications. Incoming message from Haven Control, sir."*

"Very well. Call Jalea and Tobin to the bridge.

**33**

We'll be there shortly." Nathan broke the connection before continuing. "Then we're settled on this?" Jessica shrugged in resignation. Cameron simply nodded. "Great. Let's go see what Haven Control wants."

Nathan, Cameron, and Jessica filed out of the ready room and onto the bridge just as the communications officer put the incoming message up on the loudspeaker.

*"Volander, Volander, Haven Control, please respond."* The message continued to repeat, with the exact same cadence and tone, making Nathan wonder if it was a recorded hail. He was about to respond when Jalea and Tobin entered.

"Captain," Tobin interrupted, "perhaps it would be best if I spoke with them."

Nathan looked at Jalea, who nodded, and then Jessica, who shrugged. "Very well," he agreed, stepping aside.

Tobin stepped up to the communications station, waiting for the comm officer to indicate that the channel was open and ready.

"Haven Control, this is Volander."

*"Volander, why was your response delayed?"* There was a sense of urgency in the controller's voice that worried Nathan and Jessica, both of whom were standing close by.

"Apologies, Haven, but our deep space communications array suffered damage in transit."

*"Volander, state you reasons for approach."*

"We seek to harvest from the rings and to procure supplies from your local merchants."

*"Understood. Will you require local crews?"*

"Affirmative, Volander shall require local crews."

"*Understood. Transmit your desired quotas and we will assign you a harvesting position.*"

"We will transmit our quotas shortly. Volander out." Tobin turned to face the captain. "That should do it."

"Who's Volander?" Jessica asked.

"The ship that originally used the codes entered into your transponder. It was reported missing many months ago."

"What's this 'quota' they were asking for?" Nathan inquired.

"They wish to know the amount of material we plan to harvest from the rings in order to calculate the fees that will be due them upon your departure. A few hundred kilotons is a common amount."

"Seems like a lot," Nathan observed.

"Too little, and they will be suspicious as to your true intentions. Too much, and your fees will be difficult to pay," Tobin warned.

Nathan was uneasy with the whole arrangement. He was sure that Tobin was getting far more out of the deal than he had let on. Nathan figured, for now, it was best to play along. He looked over at Jessica, whom he guessed was thinking the same thing. "Very well, transmit the amount you think best."

"Tell them our quota will be three hundred kilotons," Tobin informed the comm officer before turning back to Nathan. "That should take no more than a day or two to harvest, process, and sell on the surface to pay for your supplies."

"Can we up the amount later if needed?"

"You may, but it would probably raise undue suspicion."

"We're receiving navigational instructions, sir," the comm officer reported.

"Feed them to navigation, Ensign."

Cameron went to the navigation station and began plotting a course change. "They're sending us to a fairly dense part of the rings, Captain, not too far from the Haven colony moon itself. Should be a pretty good place to hide out for a while."

"Very well. Take us in, Cam." Nathan turned back to Tobin. "So how's this going to work, again? You're going to bring up some workers or something, and they're going to work from here?"

"No need for concern, Captain. Very few ships that come to harvest the rings bring their own harvesting equipment and crews. There are many teams available for hire on Haven. They will bring their ships and workers here. The harvester will collect material from the rings and bring it to your hangar deck. There it will be offloaded, sorted, and repackaged. Some goes to your hold. Some goes back to Haven where it will be sold to pay for your supplies, as well as the workers doing the harvesting. It is quite common, and we get ships from all over the quadrant. The material in the rings is quite rich with precious metals and water ice. It is a unique and rare combination, as you will soon see."

Nathan nodded his understanding. "Are we all set?" he asked Cameron.

"Course plotted and ready."

"I'll take us in," he insisted. "You go and take a break. Get something to eat. You're going to be in command while I'm gone, so this may be your last chance for a break for some time."

"Okay. Then I'm headed for a shower and a meal," Cameron announced as she headed out.

"That's not a bad idea," Jessica agreed. "I think I'll do the same."

"Actually," Tobin interrupted, "where we're going, being too clean might attract attention. It might be best if those going to the surface refrained from bathing until they returned."

"Okay, good to know," Nathan said.

"If there is nothing else for now, I will prepare my ship for departure," Tobin announced, stepping back toward the exit. He waited for any objections, and once satisfied there were none, spun around and headed out the door.

Nathan looked at Jalea, who had been silent the entire time. "This all sound about right to you?" he asked.

Jalea looked puzzled by his phrasing for a moment until she deduced his meaning. "This is the way it is usually done in this system," she assured him. "As long as we do nothing to attract attention, I do not expect any difficulties."

Nathan nodded his understanding as Jalea turned and followed Tobin out.

"I wish I was as confident about this plan as they seem to be," Cameron muttered as she passed. "Come on, Jessica. Let's go get something to eat."

Jessica turned to follow Cameron out. "That's gonna be a long, smelly shuttle ride," she said.


"Let's go try out some of those meal kits they retrieved," Jessica suggested as she caught up with Cameron in the corridor. She had grown tired of the nuts and dried fruit just like everyone else on board. Jessica noticed Cameron's expression. She usually had a serious look on her face, but her current expression was more serious than usual, even for Cameron. "What's bugging you?"

"I'm worried about your trip to Haven," Cameron admitted.

"Piece of cake, boss. We swoop in, do a little shopping, ask a few strategic questions, and then haul ass outta there. Standard tourist op," Jessica assured her.

"It's not you I'm worried about," Cameron told her. "It's Nathan, or more specifically, Jalea. I don't like the influence she seems to have over him. I don't trust her."

"Well, duh. Who does?"

"He does," Cameron stated.

"No, he doesn't. At least not as much as you think," Jessica insisted. "He's just playing along with her, seeing where it takes us. He's not as gullible as everyone thinks he is. He's actually pretty good at reading people."

"Yeah, I know he is. But he also tends to act too quickly, without thinking things through first. From what I'm hearing, Haven is not the kind of place where you want to be acting impulsively."

"Not to worry, Commander. I'll have his back the whole time." Jessica looked at Cameron, who said nothing. "Seriously, Cam. This is what I do, okay? He's not going down there alone, you know. He's going to have two spec-ops, a marine, and an ex-ground pounder backing him up." Cameron looked at her with a puzzled look on her face. "Oh, you didn't know? Vlad spent four years in greens before he got into the academy. So you see, you've got nothing to worry about. If any trouble starts, Haven won't know what the hell hit them!"

Cameron was a bit surprised at her enthusiasm,

unaware of Jessica's desire to do field work. "Just don't let him wander off by himself, or worse, just him and Jalea. I still don't trust her."

"You've got it, Commander. Eyes on the skipper twenty-four seven," she joked. "Wait, that's not right," she added sarcastically. How many hours are in a day down there?"

Cameron stopped in the middle of the corridor. "I mean it, Ensign." Cameron looked dead on into Jessica's eyes, obviously displeased with her levity. "You stick to him like glue. Understood?" she ordered.

Jessica straightened up, her expression becoming more serious. "Yes, sir." The two of them stood there staring at each other for a moment before Jessica finally spoke up again. "Can we go eat now?" A tiny smile began to form on the corner of Cameron's mouth, as she turned to continue down the corridor toward the mess hall.

# CHAPTER TWO

"You wanna give me a hand over here?" Nathan asked Cameron as she entered the bridge. "It's gettin' a bit crowded out there." Cameron made her way over and took a seat at the navigation console next to Nathan.

"Damn," Cameron exclaimed. She had never before seen the navigation screen with so many ship tracks displayed. "I guess the rings of Haven *are* a popular place." Nathan wasn't really listening, instead choosing to concentrate on flying the ship using the course plots Cameron was already feeding him. There were at least fifty ships in their general area, and despite the great distances between them, they were all moving fast enough that a few seconds hesitation could spell disaster.

"Suggest you maintain a considerable distance above the rings until we reach our harvesting zone," Ensign Yosef reported from the sensor station. "There are quite a few stray rocks floating just outside the normal plane of the rings, and they're a bit hard to detect until the last moment."

"How much longer until synchronous orbit?" Nathan asked.

"Two minutes," Cameron answered calmly.

"We'll come in high over our assigned parking spot. Once we sync our orbit, I'll translate down slowly into the rings."

"Copy that." Cameron closely monitored the ship's rate of deceleration, making sure the flight computer would match their forward velocity to the proper orbital velocity for their assigned altitude. Although they were still traveling at considerable speeds, in relation to the rotational speed of the gas giant below them, it was no more than a diminishing crawl.

"One minute," she announced.

"I've got a ship approaching from astern, slightly to starboard," Jessica warned. "She'll have a visual on us in five minutes."

The last thing they wanted was for other ships passing by to get a good look at them. Although the Aurora had been designed to have a less threatening appearance than the Earth's Defender-class warships, she still looked more like a warship than a freighter. Though all her weaponry was recessed into her hull and covered up when not in use, anyone with a bit of knowledge about ship design would be able to pick out her weapons' emplacements with ease. Even if they didn't, the battle scars and the huge hole in her bow would be enough to raise suspicion on its own.

"We may have to translate down faster than I'd hoped," he warned Cameron. "I think it's best if no one gets a close look at us. Not if we can avoid it."

Cameron said nothing. She knew why he wanted to duck the ship into the rings as soon as possible. The rings were just as dense as Tobin had described, and it was not something that you wanted to fly into too quickly. If someone *did* get a good look at them, and then reported what they saw to the family that controlled the Haven system, things could become a lot more dangerous than a quick drift down into the rings.

"Synchronous orbit achieved," Cameron reported.

"Scan directly below us, Kaylah," Nathan called out. "And don't be afraid to alert me if we're about to hit something big."

"Yes, sir," Ensign Yosef responded.

"Translating down." Nathan fired the docking thrusters, pushing the ship straight down toward the rings. He held the thrust far longer than usual, picking up considerably more speed in his translation than anyone could feel even remotely comfortable about, especially Cameron.

"Easy, Nathan. Back off a bit." There was genuine fear in her voice. It was unusual to hear an emotional tone from Cameron, especially during flight operations. Considering how fast they were dropping toward the rings, it was understandable, even if a bit unexpected.

"Come forward two hundred meters, quickly," Kaylah ordered. Nathan didn't ask why. The urgency in Kaylah's usually demure voice was reason enough. Nathan blasted the thrusters again, this time pushing them forward as they continued to translate downward into the rings.

"One fifty," Kaylah reported. "Come slightly starboard now."

"I see it now," Cameron reported. The moment Kaylah had barked out her recommendation, Cameron had switched her display over to track only what was nearby. Now she was starting to pick up the small and medium-sized rocks that made up the rings of Haven. "That's awfully dense, Nathan."

"How far?"

"Two kilometers. Rotate two degrees to port."

"Rotating," Nathan acknowledged as he applied a

tiny amount of thrust.

"That's good." Cameron watched as the details of the field of rocks below them began to resolve into greater clarity. "Maybe you'd better pitch down and dive in nose first."

"Our underside is thicker," Nathan objected.

"Maybe, but if we come in nose first, we've got a much better chance of not colliding with anything. And if we do, it'll be at a shallow angle instead of ninety, less likely to cause damage."

"Pitching down," he responded without hesitation. He hadn't realized it at the time, but Cameron had made the suggestion without being argumentative. He had followed her advice on instinct, without thinking twice about it.

During their training, they had been unable to work together effectively as a team. Their operational styles had been in complete conflict. Despite the assertions of Captain Roberts—that each of their strengths offset the other's weaknesses making them the perfect team—learning to work together without wanting to kill one another had been nearly impossible.

Their conflicting styles aside, the events of the last few days had forced them to put their differences aside out of necessity. They were no longer in training; they were fighting to survive. Despite the fact that circumstances had thrust Nathan into command—a fact that he was sure still bothered Cameron—it seemed they were starting to get along. *Captain Roberts would've been proud,* he thought.

"One kilometer," Cameron updated. Nathan finished pitching the nose of the Aurora downward. They were now diving nose first toward the rings below.

"How far is that ship?" Nathan asked Jessica.

"Visual in one minute," she reported.

"Will he be above or below our altitude when he reaches visual range?"

"Huh? Uh, just about even, I think." Jessica hadn't expected that question, and it had caught her slightly unprepared.

"How long until we penetrate the rings?" Nathan asked Cameron.

"About ninety seconds," she told him.

"No pressure," he muttered.

The ship continued to dive toward the rings as the unknown vessel grew closer. At this point, it was a matter of timing. They needed to get to the rings and become hidden amongst the debris before the unknown vessel got a good look at them. Nathan wanted to kick in the main drive and race into the rings, but he knew that such a move would not only be incredibly dangerous, but would also appear quite suspicious to the unknown vessel as well as anyone else that happened to be watching. Thus he was forced to run this particular race at a snail's pace compared to their usual maneuvering velocities.

"One minute," Cameron updated. "Five hundred meters."

"Unknown vessel will reach visual range in thirty seconds," Jessica reported.

"How are we looking, Kaylah?" Nathan asked, not taking his eyes off his console.

"With this narrow profile, you should be clear into the rings, sir."

"Guess you were right," Nathan mumbled. Cameron said nothing, only casting him a quick glance followed by the slightest of smirks.

"Twenty seconds to visual range," Jessica reported.

"Cam," Nathan suddenly asked, "is it okay to roll on our way in?"

"Uh, yeah, I think so. Why?"

Nathan applied a slight bit of roll thrust. "I'm gonna show them our belly as they pass," he explained, pleased with himself.

The Aurora began to roll as the unknown vessel reached visual range and passed by her. All the other ship ever saw was the Aurora's nondescript underside as she rolled over, diving into the rings.

"Penetrating rings," Cameron reported. "You can begin braking now, Nathan."

"Just a few more seconds." Although the rings were dense, they were only a kilometer thick. The last thing Nathan wanted to do was fly right through and come out the other side in front of who knew how many other ships. Finally, at the latest possible moment, he fired the braking thrusters and brought them up to full power, rapidly decreasing the ship's forward momentum until she finally came to a stop deep within the dense rings of Haven.

The entire bridge sighed collectively as Cameron reported, "Confirming all stop." Her fingers danced across her console, entering commands and calling up information. Finally she added, "We are now in synchronous orbit within the rings, on station at the assigned coordinates."

Nathan turned and rose from the helmsman's seat. "Jessica, I believe we have a flight to catch." He then turned to Cameron. "You have the ship, Commander."

"Aye, sir," Cameron answered as she watched him go. Cameron caught Jessica's eye on her way out, just in time to catch a halfhearted salute and a wink.

\* \* \*

Tobin's ship was already fired up, her engines idling in the hangar bay as Nathan and Jessica approached. Vladimir, Ensign Mendez, and Sergeant Weatherly were all standing near the ship, waiting until it was time to board. Each of them were wearing unmarked coveralls that were long overdue for the laundry, keeping in line with Tobin's suggestion to not appear too clean.

"Well, aren't we a motley looking group? Where's your guide?" Nathan asked Vladimir as he approached.

"Inside, with Tobin and Jalea," he said.

"Which one did you end up bringing?"

"Danik. Allet had no desire to go Haven. I do not think he likes the place very much."

"That's encouraging," Nathan said. Just then, Tobin descended down the boarding ramp of his ship, dropping the last half meter onto the deck.

"Is everyone here?" Tobin asked.

"Yeah. How do we look?" Nathan asked.

"Like any other freighter crew, I suspect. However, I will provide you with some cloaks to wear before we arrive. It is very common attire where we are going, as it offers an additional degree of protection against the environment on Haven. Other than all of your hair being a bit shorter than most, you should not attract undue attention."

"And I thought my hair needed a trim," Enrique joked as he followed Tobin up into the ship.

One by one, they climbed up into the long,

compact ship, with Nathan being the last one aboard. The interior was cramped, with three seats along each side of the back cabin, all facing inward. There was a hatch on the back bulkhead that led to a small cargo hold and another hatch at the front end that led to the cockpit.

Nathan took his seat by the cargo hatch on the opposite side of the cabin next to Jalea. The seats themselves were rather firm and not very comfortable, obviously not designed for a long journey. They also had some type of restraint system built into them, the belts appearing to have seen better days. Looking forward into the cockpit, Nathan could see that Tobin was not bothering to put on his restraints, so Nathan assumed that none of them would need theirs either. The fact that Jalea also did not feel the need to restrain herself only served to support his decision.

The sound of the idling engines became louder as the exterior hatch swung up and closed, sealing with a hiss of compressed air. Once closed, the whine of the engines was greatly reduced. However, the vibrations inside the ship told of the increasing strain on her engines as the small ship began rolling, making a U-turn to port and heading into the transfer airlock.

Nathan could see out the window built into the hatch on the opposite wall, watching as the frame of the airlock moved past them. Through the front windows of the cockpit, he could see the outer airlock door. It would take only a few minutes for the airlock to purge itself of pressure, and then the outer door would open and the transfer airlock would become one with the vacuum of space.

Again, the small ship began to roll. Nathan

watched out the side window as the ship moved out of the transfer airlock and out into the outer bay, eventually coming completely into the open only a few meters from the aft edge of the flight deck. As they came out from under the canopy and into the open, the light reflecting off the reddish-brown and orange gas giant outside washed into the cabin, bathing them all in its eerie glow.

The little ship fired its thrusters, quickly climbing away from the Aurora and slightly to her starboard. The sound of her landing gear as it retracted up into the ship was unusually loud, as was the *clunk* that was heard when the gear locked into place. As they accelerated away, Nathan could see the numerous chunks that had been carved out of the Aurora's outer hull by the many hits she had sustained during her recent battles with both the Jung and the Takaran. The sight of the damage to her exterior made Nathan ill, and he found himself thankful that they hadn't flown over the port side of the ship where there was a huge hull breach in her bow.

Chunks of rock and ice of varying sizes and shapes drifted past them as they made their way down and out of the rings. Within only a few minutes of leaving the Aurora, the small ship had cleared the rings and was headed for the large moon called Haven. As they followed along the underside of the immense field of debris, Nathan and the others could see different ships conducting their own harvesting operations. They were of different shapes and sizes, ranging from not much bigger than the one they were on to some larger than their own Defender-class warships back in Sol.

Nathan could feel his pulse quicken, his heart beating in his throat as he gazed out the windows of the small ship. He had left the familiarity of his own ship to hitch a ride in this tiny, alien spacecraft. He was a thousand light years from home, seeing things that the people of his world could only dream about. Nathan looked over at Vladimir. He too was staring out the window in disbelief, along with everyone else in the cabin.

"This is unbelievable," Nathan mumbled.

"There are so many different ships!" Vladimir exclaimed.

"Yeah, and all of them better armed," Jessica added. "You two might want to keep it under control a bit," she mumbled, looking toward the cockpit to see if Tobin had overheard them. "No point letting on what 'newbs' we are out here." Jessica shot a look at Nathan and Vladimir, reinforcing her warning. For a moment, Nathan felt incredibly naive. Vladimir simply shrugged it off and continued gazing out the window.

"Hey, you notice that none of the big ships come anywhere near Haven?" Sergeant Weatherly observed as they approached the large brown and blue moon. "Only the little ones."

"Most of the big ones are cargo ships," Nathan explained. "They probably don't have the power to change orbits frequently, especially when they're fully loaded. It makes piloting them a bit trickier. You have to be very efficient, conserve every bit of momentum and fuel. Look at their main engines. They're mostly just small engines with considerable fuel storage behind them, designed to do long, low-level burns."

"Is that why the Aurora's got such a big ass?" Enrique joked.

"Yeah, actually. And her ass is all engine, too.

She can really get up and move in a hurry."

"Enrique likes big asses that can move," Jessica smiled, nudging her spec-op partner.

"Is that right?" Nathan said.

"Yeah, that's why I never hit on you," Enrique jabbed back. "You don't have an ass!"

"Not a big one, that's for sure," she corrected.

Nathan smiled, thinking of that night a few weeks ago, back on Earth. The memory of her reflection in the mirrored wall tile as she had pulled her dress back on brought a slight smile to his face.

"We will begin our descent momentarily," Tobin called back from the cockpit. "It will get a little rough as we hit the atmosphere. The inertial dampeners on this little ship are not terribly effective, I'm afraid."

"Thanks for the warning," Nathan called back. "I'm sure we'll be fine."

Most of the shuttle rides that Nathan had taken to and from the orbit of Earth during his academy days had been in the older shuttles that had no inertial dampeners. The first few rides had been frightening. He had never quite gotten used to them, but he had learned to tolerate them. The worst part had always been the plasma wakes. The white-orange fire streaking past the windows as the shuttles plowed through the thickening atmosphere was the scary part. It always seemed as if the fire would burst through the cabin at any moment and consume them all.

The ship rolled slightly, giving them a better view as they made their way around the moon. Haven was about half the size of Earth, and from orbit, it appeared different in many respects. Most notable was its color. It was mostly brown with some patches of gray and green. The surface was mostly dry land, broken up occasionally by a few large bodies of water that paled in comparison to the oceans on Earth. There appeared to be a few mountain ranges, some small oddly colored forests, and a lot of open plains. There were even snow-covered poles. Most of the surface appeared to be barren of life. And what plant life there was appeared odd from orbit, paler somehow. Many of the plains appeared to be covered with a tan-colored substance. The color reminded him of sandy beaches back on Earth. But there were no large bodies of water near the big tan splotches that Nathan could see.

He could see a few active volcanoes, complete with large lava flows. On first impression, it seemed an odd mixture of both the hospitable and the hellish.

The moon grew considerably larger in the windows until it was alarmingly close. "Shouldn't we have rolled back over by now?" Nathan commented. He was the only pilot among them. Therefore, he was answered with blank stares.

A moment later, something began humming loudly from the compartment behind them. A few seconds after that, a strange bluish glow seemed to envelope the ship.

"Some kind of shielding?" Vladimir guessed.

The ship began to vibrate and bounce slightly as the bluish-white field surrounding the ship began to change color, taking on a more amber hue. Within a minute, the bouncing had become more violent and the field surrounding them was glowing a bright yellow-orange that had become so intense it all but blocked their view of the world below.

"I think it's a heat shield," Nathan told them.

"Is that even possible?" Vladimir asked.

"I guess so. That would explain why we didn't

need to pitch over."

It seemed impossible to Nathan. Every space-faring vessel he had ever seen had a heat protective layer along its underside. Even the Aurora's underside was reinforced and heat-shielded in order to allow for limited atmospheric flight as well as for aero-braking maneuvers. But such materials usually added to the mass of a ship as well as to the complexity and expense of her production. If these people did have an energy-based shield to protect them against the extreme friction of atmospheric entry, it would be a highly useful technology to bring back to Earth. The applications would be endless.

His contemplations of how such a technology could be used were interrupted by the increasingly violent shaking of the little ship. Despite the shield that prevented the heat of entry from reaching them, it apparently did little to reduce the turbulence. It seemed even worse than he remembered from his last re-entry to Earth. One of the things he had always liked about space was that there was no turbulence. Nathan hated turbulence, which was surprising considering that a large part of his training at the academy had been spent learning to fly every type of aircraft known to the people of his world. That turbulence, however, had not bothered him since he had been the pilot. Right now, as a passenger, he was feeling it in the pit of his stomach.

He scanned the faces of his team. Moments ago they had been joking with one another. Now, they all had rather serious looks on their faces as they too wondered if the ship was going to hold together.

A few minutes later, it ended nearly as quickly as it had begun. The energy shield faded back to amber, and then to bluish-white, until it finally faded away completely with the hum of what must have been the shield generators going silent immediately thereafter.

Sometime during the entry, Tobin had rolled the ship back over, and now they were properly oriented in relation to the world below. They were a few thousand meters above what appeared to be a small inland sea, heading toward a distant shore stretched out before them. The ship continued to gradually descend as it approached the shoreline. Minutes later they were over land, down to only a few hundred meters and still descending. They could see various farms and ranches below, broken up by the occasional cluster of buildings. They were headed toward a large city of some sort.

The tan splotches that had resembled beaches from orbit now appeared to be some large flat plant that in some cases covered hundreds of square meters of land. Nathan couldn't tell if it was all one plant or many plants grown together. He also noticed people cutting the flat plant up into smaller pieces and tossing them onto the back of large, flat vehicles.

The farms quickly disappeared, giving way to more urban concerns. They continued their descent until they were only a hundred meters off the ground on their final approach to the spaceport. Nathan could hear Tobin talking in an official tone to someone over his headset, and he assumed it was some type of air-traffic controller. After all, the sky over the spaceport was full of ships coming and going, and someone had to be telling them all what to do.

From above, the space port appeared to be a hodgepodge of parking stalls, hangars, and service buildings, all connected by various runways, taxiways, landing pads, and service roadways. There was a complex at roughly the center of the airfield with numerous auxiliary buildings clustered around what appeared to be the main terminal building. Similar in overall design and function to the numerous spaceports of Earth, this one appeared to have started small and expanded over time. Dissimilar to the ones on Earth, this facility was right in the center of the city, as if the city had grown up around it. Nathan could see homes and businesses with their backs right up against the spaceport, and he wondered how anyone could function so near to all the commotion and noise that the facility must generate.

Finally, the ship slowed, pivoted right, and began its final descent to their assigned landing point, her engines screaming as they strained to keep the small ship aloft. Nathan could hear the sound of the landing gear as it extended from the ship. A moment later, the ship bounced gently onto a landing pad made of a large, extremely robust grate that was elevated a couple meters above the ground to allow for the thrust wash of their engines. The moment they touched down, the ship's engines immediately spun down to a low whine.

The ship rolled off the landing pad onto the tarmac, winding its way between rows of parking stalls. Most were open stalls with nothing more than service buildings separating them on either side, while others had roofs over them. On approach, he had seen rows of hangars, but the area they were in did not appear to have any such buildings.

Nathan peered out the window as they rolled past dozens of spacecraft, many of which didn't look like they could make it to orbit. Some of the spacecraft were being made ready for departure. Others were being serviced. While a few appeared to have been out of commission for some time. There were even a few that had temporary fences locked around them, presumably to prevent access to them for whatever reason. In light of what Tobin had said about the family that controlled Haven, Nathan wondered if the owners of the locked-down spacecraft had failed to pay tribute and lost access to their vessels as a result.

Several minutes later, the ship turned sharply and rolled in between two long service buildings. Nathan could see a couple of men in dirty coveralls peering out the window of one of the buildings, watching them as they rolled to a stop and shut down their engines. Moments later, Tobin removed his headset and began to climb out of his seat. "Welcome to Haven," he announced as he left the cockpit.

Tobin pushed past them as he made his way to the rear of the cabin. He punched in a code on the keypad next to the door on the back bulkhead, and it slid open to reveal a small corridor that led to another hatch farther back with storage racks on either side. Nathan and the others watched as Tobin reached for a group of light brown cloaks hung on the wall.

"Whoa!" Jessica yelled, as she jumped from her seat, drawing her sidearm and taking aim at Tobin. "Hands where I can see them!" she added, her weapon now fully trained on Tobin. Enrique was only a step behind her, his weapon also drawn, with Sergeant Weatherly right behind him.

"What the hell?" Nathan exclaimed. It appeared that every member of his team, including Vladimir, had their weapons drawn. Nathan seemed to be the only one of them that did not. "Something I should know, guys?"

"Step back!" Jessica ordered. "Hands high!" Tobin, with his hands held in plain sight, stepped back from the cloaks, turning to face Jessica as he slowly raised his open hands.

"I was only reaching for the cloaks," Tobin insisted in his most charming and innocent tone. "I assure you."

Jessica peeked over her shoulder to verify that the rest of her team were prepared to back her up. She stepped forward, grabbing Tobin by the collar and spinning him around before shoving him up against the wall. Enrique shifted to his left, getting a better angle from which to keep his weapon trained on Tobin without Jessica being in his line of fire.

"What is it?" Nathan inquired, standing to try and get a better view.

Jessica turned around, pushing the cloaks to one side to reveal a gun rack containing dozens of handguns, assault rifles, grenades, and what looked like shoulder-fired rocket launchers. "I thought you said you weren't armed." Jessica challenged Tobin.

"I said *I* wasn't armed when we first met in your hangar bay," Tobin defended. "I did not claim that I owned no weapons."

"Uh huh," Jessica mumbled as she inspected his hidden arsenal. "Do a lot of hunting, I suppose?"

"Nathan," Jalea protested, "if your security personnel are going to react so violently at the slightest possible threat, we are all in for a very difficult time here on Haven. I assure you, most of Haven's residents are far less tolerant of such behavior."

"I apologize," Nathan responded. "But in the interests of all our safety, you might want to tell us now if there are any other *weapons* you might have hidden on board."

Jessica gestured to the others to stand down, as she too holstered her weapon. Tobin turned to face Nathan, his hand slowly coming back down to his sides as he spoke. "This is my entire stock," he promised. "They are only for defensive purposes."

"Defensive purposes?" Jessica questioned. "Against what, a battalion?" Jessica handed him the pile of cloaks he had originally been after, gesturing for him to exit the compartment before her.

"You would be surprised at how much *defensive* armament can be required on Haven," Jalea said.

Tobin began handing out cloaks to each of them. "I would suggest that you wear these cloaks at all times during your visit. They are common here and will serve to protect you from the environment. They will also help you to hide your weapons from view, as well as help you to blend in amongst the crowds."

Nathan accepted the last cloak as Tobin stepped past him. The cloak was made of a thick yet lightweight fabric that had obviously not been washed in some time and smelled rather unpleasant.

Tobin cracked open the hatch, which swung downward toward the tarmac. Small steps extruded from the hatch itself as it neared the deck, stopping about fifty centimeters from the dull gray surface outside.

The cabin quickly filled with the heavy, humid air of Haven. An unusual smell, a mixture of mechanical fluids and a pungent, musky odor, immediately hit Nathan. The aroma was almost overpowering at first but soon subsided. After nearly a month living in the scrubbed, temperature-controlled air of their ship, the natural atmosphere, no matter how aromatic, was a welcome change.

Tobin was the first one out, moving gingerly down the boarding ramp and dropping the last step down. Being nearest the hatch, Nathan was next to exit the ship. He stepped out onto the ramp, standing tall in the open air. The sky was a pale, unnatural-looking amber. He realized why their entry into the atmosphere had been so turbulent, as he could feel the increased air pressure of this moon. It was somewhat warm and quite humid, as if it would begin to rain at any moment.

Nathan looked around briefly. They were parked between two long metal-clad service buildings. The buildings themselves were obviously cheap and easy to construct, with few doors and windows and a single roll-up cargo door. Looking forward and aft, he could see they were at least several rows back from either side of the berthing yard. He caught sight of plenty of activity, with people moving about their various ships, and service vehicles cruising between the rows of stalls.

He looked up at the sky. Its subdued amber was almost like the sky on Earth just after the sun had dropped below the horizon. But this world's sun was still sitting low in her sky. It was small and pale compared to their sun back on Earth, and it provided considerably less light than he had expected. Nathan could even look directly at it for several seconds without hurting his eyes. In the opposite direction of the sun, the gas giant around that the moon of Haven orbited filled the bottom half of the sky from the ground upward. The light reflecting off the gas giant provided a secondary light source, casting fainter shadows in the opposite direction of those cast by Haven's sun. The effect was wholly unnatural, and it gave the entire scene an eerie cast.

Nathan made his way down the ramp, dropping the last step onto the tarmac. His landing felt light, as if he had jumped down only a fraction of the actual distance. The gravity here was only half that of his home world, and a quarter less than the Aurora's standard gravity. He jumped up and down a few times, finding himself coming considerably farther off the ground than he would have expected under normal circumstances. It was an unusual sensation—both frightening and exhilarating at the same time—which brought a boyish grin to his face.

"You know, Nathan, you are probably the first person from Earth to set foot on another world in over a millennium," Vladimir told him as he dropped to the tarmac next to him.

"Guess I should have said something profound, huh?"

"What the hell is that smell?" Jessica asked as she stepped off the ramp.

"Not exactly profound," Nathan mumbled, "but accurate." Vladimir chuckled as he bounced up and down, bounding a few steps away from the ship as he too experimented with the reduced gravity.

"This area is covered with an edible fungus," Tobin explained. "It is everywhere there is dirt, and it can be rather pungent. It is, however, very flavorful and nutritious. It has in fact made civilization possible on this moon, as it grows with almost no effort and is quite a profitable commodity. Although it is not as appreciated on other worlds as much as those that grow it would've hoped."

"What time of day is it here?" Nathan asked Tobin.

"It is midday."

"Really? It looks more like sunset."

"We are late in our light cycle."

"Light cycle?"

"While Haven is passing between the star and the planet, there are fifty-two days of normal day and night. When we pass behind the planet, there is only darkness for the following fifty-two days."

"No sun for fifty-two days?" Jessica asked rhetorically. "How depressing."

"One becomes accustomed to it over time," Tobin commented nonchalantly.

"Explains the abundance of fungus," Jessica mumbled.

"So what happens next?" Nathan asked.

"We must go to one of the labor halls. There we can hire a crew to do the harvesting for you. The sooner this is begun, the sooner you will have funds with which to purchase the goods you require."

"Lead the way," Nathan invited.

"Transportation should arrive momentarily. So, Ensign," Tobin said, looking at Jessica, "if you could refrain from shooting them, it would be appreciated. It is a long walk to the main terminal area."

"I'll try to control myself," she promised.

"I must caution you all," Tobin continued as he raised the hood on his cloak to cover his head, "to use discretion while on Haven. Keep covered up as much as possible when outside to protect yourself from the elements. Although the sun does not appear strong, it does deposit considerable radiation on our little world. The fibers of these cloaks are designed to reflect much of this radiation. And do not attract attention to yourselves. Most of the people here are not residents of this world. Therefore, they are as apprehensive as you are about their own security. It would serve you well to remember this."

"Are you suggesting that we don't defend ourselves?" Jessica challenged. She knew that he was not; she just wanted him to understand that she wasn't about to let anything happen to them.

"Of course not, Ensign. Just think twice before pulling your weapon," he suggested as he turned to lead them away.

"Thinking twice is usually a good way to get yourself killed," Enrique commented to Jessica under his breath.

"Yeah, that's exactly what I was thinking," she agreed. "Listen, you and Weatherly take the rear. You try to soak up as much intel as you can while you watch our six."

"Got it," Enrique acknowledged.

"Sarge, you keep your eyes on Danik."

"What're you going to be doing?" Enrique asked.

"I'll be watching Tobin," she told them, as their transportation arrived. "I don't trust that skinny little shit."

\* \* \*

The ride through the spaceport had been brief, having moved along at a good speed. But traveling the short distance from the spaceport to the labor hall had been anything but. The spaceport was the center of all commerce and activity on the small world. During the ride, Tobin had informed them that most of Haven was still undeveloped. The moon had only been colonized a few decades ago to provide support for increased harvesting of the rings. It was because of this that Haven City—the only city on this world—had spread out in all directions from its sole spaceport.

After exiting the main gate, they had only needed to travel less than a kilometer down one of the many roads leading away from the spaceport. From what they had seen, each of these main roads was lined with shops and offices of various interests. There were also all manner of street vendors peddling their modest wares. Nathan guessed that they could probably purchase everything they needed by spending a few days shopping in these congested lanes.

After spending considerable time working their way slowly down the boulevard, they arrived at a large, tan building. It was dirty and its exterior was in considerable disrepair. There were many men and a few women lingering about outside. A large sign over the massive double doors identified the purpose of the building in a language that Nathan could not decipher. By the looks of the men milling about, however, he was pretty sure they had arrived at the labor hall.

"It would not be wise for all of us to enter the hall," Tobin instructed as they dismounted the vehicle. "Perhaps only a few?"

"Jessica?" Nathan asked, seeking her read on the situation.

"The four of us go in," she suggested, gesturing at Tobin, Jalea, Nathan, and herself. "The others can look around out here."

"Perhaps four is too many." Tobin urged. "I was thinking perhaps just you and I..."

"Where the captain goes, I go," Jessica

interrupted. The determined look in her eyes told Tobin that it would be pointless to argue.

"I see. Then perhaps the three of us…"

"Jalea is my interpreter," Nathan insisted.

Tobin sighed in acquiescence. "Very well, the four of us it is." He bowed his head slightly and extended his arm toward the main door, inviting them to enter.

"Sounds good," Nathan agreed. He was definitely out of his comfort zone, and felt better having Jessica—who had proven herself in combat on more than one occasion—deciding how to best keep them safe in this unfamiliar land. He turned to Tobin again. "How long do you think we'll be in here?"

"It depends on how many bidders are still looking for work today," he explained. "This late in the day, however, I expect our choices to be few."

"Don't you love how he answers a question without actually answering it?" Jessica muttered to Nathan under her breath, raising a slight smile on his face. It was something he had already noticed about the man during their first meeting.

"Okay," Jessica spoke up, turning to face Enrique and the others. "We're going inside this big ugly building here. Should be a hoot. You four take a look around out here. But stay close, and keep your ears on. I have no idea how long we'll be, or how quickly we'll be looking to move out when we're done. So stay flexed and ready."

"You got it, Jess," Enrique answered. Vladimir and Danik had already headed away toward the nearest shop that appeared to deal in some type of technology. Enrique turned to follow, gesturing for Sergeant Weatherly to join him.

"Lead the way," Nathan told Tobin.

Tobin turned and headed up the steps to the building with Jalea, Nathan, and Jessica following. He entered the hall, removing his hood on the way in, and bowed to the gruff-looking man behind the front counter. After a brief exchange with the clerk, Tobin gestured for them to follow him deeper into the hall. "I informed the clerk that we were looking to hire a harvesting crew. He informed me that there are a few crews still available, so the bidding should be quick."

They followed Tobin into the main hall. The room was large and open, with high-beamed ceilings. There were large heavy wooden tables and benches lined up throughout the room. It looked as if it could accommodate hundreds of workers when filled to capacity. At the moment, there were only a half dozen teams remaining, each represented by at least two leaders.

The clerk delivered a small electronic tablet to a man sitting behind a large desk on a raised platform at one corner of the room. Nathan assumed it was a data device similar to those they used on the Aurora. He watched as the man read the small pad, preparing to perform his part of the hiring ritual. About the room, the various team leaders noticed their entrance, as well as the arrival of the clerk. Nathan realized these events had alerted them to the presence of a new employment opportunity, and each of them appeared to be preparing themselves to bid.

The large man behind the desk gestured for Tobin to approach, exchanging words with him. A moment later, the man spoke through the loudspeaker. "The Volonese cargo ship Volander wishes to hire a harvesting crew," the man announced. "Expected quota is three hundred kilotons. Completion time is two days. Payment desired is ten percent minus fees and expenses." The man paused, giving the team leaders a chance to crunch their numbers and prepare their bids. After a minute, he continued. "The bidding is open."

"Twenty-five! Plus fees and expenses!" the first team leader called out. Tobin's face crinkled, his brow furrowed in disgust at the first offer.

"Twenty-two, plus!" the second team countered. Tobin's expression failed to change.

"Twenty, plus!" the third team chimed in turn. Nathan was struck at the order in which they were bidding, wondering how it had been decided.

"Eighteen, plus!" the fourth team announced. Still Tobin's expression remained unchanged. There was a moment of silence as everyone waited for the fifth and final team to announce their bid. But the fifth team leader simply waived his hand, indicating a pass on his turn to bid. He appeared either uninterested or unwilling to commit to a bid so early in the process.

"Sixteen, plus!" the first team re-bid.

"Fifteen, plus!"

"Thirteen, plus!"

Again, the bidding got to the fifth team, and again they waived their turn. The turn then went to back to the first team, who paused, and then indicated that they were no longer interested in the job, the bid having gone below what they were prepared to work for. In a show of solidarity, the other teams also indicated they were done bidding. Tobin shook his head and returned to the side of the room to rejoin Nathan and the others.

"What happened?" Nathan asked, confused. "I

thought we needed to hire a crew."

"Patience, Captain," Tobin smiled as he strolled past them and headed toward the exit. "The negotiations have not yet concluded."

Nathan turned to follow Tobin, still unsure of what was going on. He looked at Jalea, who remained stone-faced as usual as she walked away.

Moments later, they found themselves outside the labor hall, walking down the steps.

"What the hell was all that for?" Nathan inquired, hoping for more of an explanation now that they were outside and away from the locals.

"It is all part of the ritual, Captain. Each of us must play our role in the ceremony," Tobin assured him.

"So, you're saying that..."

"You don't look Volonese," a voice called from behind him.

Nathan turned to see a small man, barely twenty years of age. His hair was shaggy, with most of it tied back in a pony tail. He wore the customary cloak and was preparing to pull the hood up over his head to protect himself against the Haven sun's unusual radiation.

Nathan recognized the man as having been in the hall earlier, sitting near the leader of the fifth team. "We don't?" Nathan responded. Tobin flashed Nathan a stern look as a caution against conversing.

"You're too clean," the man continued as he came out of the shadow cast by the building. "Volonese almost never shave. And their women are usually fat and ugly," he added, eyeing Jessica as he spoke.

"We're going for a new look," Nathan joked, ignoring Tobin's warning.

"Is there something we can do for you?" Tobin

interjected, hoping to take over the exchange to prevent Nathan from saying something unwise.

"We'll take the job," the man announced.

"At eight percent, minus fees and expenses?"

"I believe your price was ten."

"Ah, but you seek to circumvent payment to the labor hall, do you not?" Tobin countered.

"As do you," the little man pointed out. "And I am the only one out here offering to take the job, sans the labor hall's fee." It was obvious that the young man was not new at this type of wheeling and dealing. Nathan found the process intriguing.

"My mistake. Ten it was," Tobin conceded. "And you can meet the terms of delivery? It is a rather fast job, considering the quota."

"It will not be a problem. We've got the best harvester pilot on all of Haven," the man boasted.

"Forgive me—I do not intend offense—but you seem a bit young for this job."

"Possibly, but maybe that's why we're willing to take the job for the measly rate you're offering," the man smiled. He obviously didn't care if he was being offensive, which made Nathan want to hire him all the more.

Tobin bowed his head in deference, refusing to take offense at the man's rebut. "Perhaps. Then it is agreed. I assume your crew is ready to begin work immediately."

"No choice, not if we wanna complete the job in two days."

"Then have one of your representatives join me at berth four-thirteen for the ride up," Tobin explained.

"You people aren't going?" the young man asked, as he circled slowly around them, paying particular attention to Jessica as he passed.

"They have other business to conduct before returning to their ship."

"Uh huh." The man smiled as he passed Jessica. "Shame. You definitely ain't from Volon." He grinned.

Nathan smiled. He definitely liked this guy.

"Find anything interesting?" Nathan asked his friend as they returned to Tobin's vehicle.

"Interesting, yes, but not useful," Vladimir said. "But the day is still young, and Danik tells me there is very large open market where they sell used components for small spacecraft. It is on other side of the spaceport."

"Captain," Tobin called. He had finished making plans with the young man representing the harvesting team and had rejoined them. "I must return to my ship and escort the harvesting crew and their ships back to yours."

"Their *ships*?" Nathan inquired, a bit surprised by the inference of multiple spacecraft.

"These teams usually have at least two or three small ships. One harvester that collects material from the rings and delivers it back to your ship, and one or two cargo shuttles to haul equipment and workers, as well as to ferry some of the harvested material back to Haven for resale in order to collect your payment and theirs. I have instructed them to use at least two ships for hauling the ore back to Haven, as I expect you will require significant resources with which to purchase the supplies you desire."

"Sir," Jessica interrupted, "I'd recommend we send Ensign Mendez and Sergeant Weatherly back to the ship with them. I'd feel better if Enrique kept an eye on the harvesting operations in my absence."

"Very well," Nathan agreed. "Tobin, can you take two of my people back with you?"

"Of course, Captain. I should return to Haven within a few hours at the most. Meanwhile, might I suggest that you spend some time in our street markets? Perhaps try some of our local cuisine. You may find something you wish to purchase for use on your vessel. I'm sure Jalea will serve as an adequate guide in my absence, as this is not her first time on Haven."

"You don't mind?" Nathan asked Jalea, not wanting to assume her assistance would be so forthcoming.

"It would be my pleasure, Captain." Jalea smiled, placing her hand on his forearm to lead him toward the street market.

Vladimir watched as they strolled past him, a smirk on his face. He looked over at Jessica, who bore a suspicious look that somehow made Vladimir's smirk magically disappear. Sensing the tension, Vladimir decided to follow Nathan and Jalea, along with Danik.

"You two head back to the ship with Tobin," Jessica ordered Enrique and Sergeant Weatherly. "I need you to handle security on board while I'm down here. Who knows how many of these *workers* you're gonna have running around the flight deck. So keep your eyes open, and recruit anyone you need from the crew to help you. Do *not* let them beyond the flight deck. Understood?"

"No problem, Jess," Enrique answered. "Come on, Sarge. Let's mount up," he told him as he climbed into the vehicle.

# CHAPTER THREE

Nathan and Jalea strolled casually down the crowded promenade with Jessica, Vladimir, and Danik close behind. The wide lane was paved with something similar to concrete, the exact composition of which seemed a bit rockier than what was widely used on Earth. There were vendor booths lining the streets with small shops of varying types directly behind them. Some of the booths were independent of the shops, while others were merely extensions of the businesses behind them.

The crowd was thick with all manner of people, some buyers and some sellers. There were women shopping for their families with men standing by their sides. There were crews from various ships, all looking to buy needed goods and services. They all had the same, impoverished look about them, as if they had always been forced to make do with not enough.

Nathan had grown up in a family of means. They had been one of both wealth and power for as many generations as they could trace. His father's father had been a prominent politician, as had his father before him. Nathan knew that it had been a point of contention between himself and his father. Like all good sons had done since the time of the great bio-digital plague, Nathan's father had expected him to follow in his footsteps and serve in elected office. But the changes that the Data Ark had sparked back on Earth had made the concept of the family line of succession obsolete in most circles. Structured education had once again replaced long apprenticeships in all the industrialized nations on Earth. Nathan, having grown up in such an environment, had therefore felt little compulsion to continue the family trade. In fact, he had grown to despise everything about it.

Not wanting to draw attention to himself, Nathan fought to control his excitement at all of the new sights, sounds, and smells he was experiencing. The setting, although familiar in its design and intent, was at the same time completely foreign to him. Despite the fact that most people spoke Angla, there was still a dizzying array of languages being spoken. Haven was a community of migrants who came and went with the work. Jalea had told him that less than ten percent of the population was actually born and raised on the little moon. Those that were rarely lived out their lives here. Instead, most sought escape to more prosperous worlds with the prospect of brighter futures.

No matter which direction his eyes wandered, they caught glimpses of the cultural diversity that was Haven. Of even greater fascination was that these people had come from different worlds—from different *star systems*. His world had only begun to regain a sense of global community a century ago when the Data Ark had been discovered. So the idea that such a thing could exist on an *interstellar* scale was truly amazing. It actually gave him *hope* for the future of humanity. They had known that humans from Earth had built thriving civilizations on what was then referred to as the *Core Worlds*—systems within fifty light years of Sol. There had also been about a dozen lesser *fringe* worlds in development at the time the plague had swept through the core. But to his knowledge, there had never been any human colonies established beyond one hundred light years from Sol, let alone over a thousand. There had been some indications, through news footage stored in the Ark's data banks, that a wave of unauthorized colonization attempts had occurred during the early days of the plague. Scholars studying the data had theorized that such attempts had occurred as the infrastructure of the core systems collapsed, and people that were yet uninfected had simply tried to flee, hoping to start over on pristine worlds. There had been dozens of habitable worlds charted by deep space exploration vessels and by long-range detection systems. But again, they had all been within, at most, a few hundred light years.

Yet still, here they were, walking amongst humans who were the descendants of those very refugees that had fled the core so long ago. It was mind-boggling. Nathan wondered how the scholars back on Earth would react to this revelation. He wondered how it would affect his own history professor, Bill Jenkins, with whom Nathan had become close friends during his time as an undergraduate. They had spent many hours discussing just such theories, sometimes into the wee hours of the morning. Nathan was sure that being out here, witnessing all of this, would have delighted old Professor Williams to no end.

As they wandered farther through the crowds, they moved beyond the everyday trinkets and wares commonly found nearest the spaceport. They came upon a small booth selling some sort of cooked vegetable. It had a peculiar yet enticing aroma that drew Nathan to it. The smell of the vegetable as it seared in the large iron skillet of hot oil made his mouth water.

"What is this?" Nathan asked Jalea.

"That is called *pompa root*," she said. "It is cooked in the oil of the *tekatta*."

"Tekatta?"

"A small animal that lives in the ground. They are many on Haven. The farmers despise them, as they damage their crops."

"And what is that?" he asked, pointing to a stack of small, cooked squares of an off-white substance. They were almost tan in color, and also looked like they had been seared in similar fashion.

"It is called *molo*. It grows in great abundance here."

"Is that the tan stuff we saw all over the place as we flew in?"

"I believe so, yes. It is a fungus that does very well in the long darkness that befalls Haven once every orbit. It is used in most of the local dishes eaten here on Haven. It is very nutritious, although some do not care for its taste or texture."

An old woman behind the counter offered Nathan a small dish with a taste of both the pompa root and the molo, topped with a thick orange gelatinous sauce. "A taste for you, sir?" she offered.

Nathan graciously accepted the sample, plucking the pompa root from the dish and biting it. "Mmm, not bad. It tastes like a mild onion."

"Try the molo, with the sauce," Jalea suggested.

Nathan picked up the molo next, scooping up some of the gelatinous orange goop that lay beneath it. After sniffing it, he popped it into his mouth and began to chew tentatively. After a moment, his curious expression changed to one of approval. "That's pretty good. Kind of a cross between a mushroom and tofu," he explained, forgetting that Jalea would not know of any of the foods her was using for comparison. "And the sauce is like a spicy orange marmalade. Hey, Vlad!" he called out. "You've gotta try this!" Nathan turned to the old woman, about to indicate that he wanted to order five dishes of their food, when he realized that he had no way to pay her. He looked at Jalea, a bit embarrassed. "How do we pay her?"

"Allow me," Jalea offered. She placed an order in the local language, immediately being handed five larger dishes filled with a mixture similar to what Nathan had just sampled. After receiving the orders, Jalea handed the woman some small, dark gray chips, gesturing for her to accept what was probably an overpayment on Jalea's part. The old woman bowed her head respectively, thanking Jalea for her generosity.

Having all been reduced to eating dehydrated emergency rations for the last two days, they eagerly devoured the dishes of food. Vladimir, who Nathan had come to realize would eat just about anything, inhaled his portion with his usual rapidity. Danik and Jalea, both being familiar with the local cuisine, consumed their portions without hesitation. Jessica, however, did not appear as enthusiastic as the others.

"What's the matter, Jess?" Nathan asked. "Don't like your molo?" he asked with a grin.

"Tastes kind of like mushrooms," she stated, trying not to complain.

"Yeah, and tofu," Nathan exclaimed, obviously enjoying his serving much more than Jessica.

"Not exactly crazy about either one of those," she stated, forcing herself to tolerate the unusual taste and texture of the molo. "You sure this stuff is safe for us to eat?"

"Delicious!" Vladimir announced, scooping up the last of the orange sauce with his fingers. "It reminds me of the cooked cabbage my grandmother used to make."

"Maybe we should buy some of this molo, take it up to the ship, and have it analyzed. How well does it keep?" Nathan asked Jalea. He was met with a look of bewilderment. "Does it go bad quickly? Does it need to be refrigerated or something?"

"Ah, no. It is usually dried in the sun or in dehydrators. Then it remains safe to eat for a very long time. Some people will season it before dehydration and consume it later while still in its dried state."

"Molo jerky," Nathan joked. Again, Jalea was bewildered. "What do you think, Vlad?"

"What is this jerky?" Vladimir asked.

"You know, jerky. Dried strips of seasoned meat?" Nathan looked at Vladimir, who showed no sign of understanding. "Really? You've never heard of jerky?" Nathan shook off Vladimir's ignorance of the concept, turning back to Jalea. "So, maybe we could buy some molo here."

"These people only sell individual cooked servings, as do most vendors in this area. Perhaps farther down we will find someone selling larger amounts of fresh molo."

"Lead the way, then," Nathan agreed, turning to the old woman. "Thank you. It was very good," he complimented, nodding respectfully as he placed his empty dish on the counter.

They spent the next half hour winding their way casually through the crowds of shoppers, trying to move in much the same manner as the locals in order to blend in, just as Tobin had recommended. The street market reminded Nathan of the week he had spent with his academy roommate Luis in his village in South America. They had spent an afternoon meandering about a street market much like this one. It had been the first time that Nathan had traveled outside of a large metropolitan area, and it had been quite a culture shock for him. Back then, despite the fact that it had still been on his home world, it had been a totally alien environment to him. He found it surprising that this market—a thousand light years distant—felt no more alien to him than that village in South America had a few short years ago.

They stopped a few more times along the way, sampling more of the local cuisine. As Jalea had told them, everything they tried seemed to have molo in it as a staple. There had been very little variety in the available ingredients used, but their culinary creativity did not seem impaired by the lack thereof.

Jessica had expressed concern over Nathan's willingness to sample just about everything he came across, despite Doctor Chen's recommendations to the contrary. Nathan had dismissed her concerns, likening it to a trip to another country back on Earth. He had further supported his lack of caution to the fact that the ship was nearly out of food, and he doubted they could wait for the already overworked physician to complete a complex analysis of all the consumables found on this world.

"Who are the goons?" Jessica asked, spying a pair of burly men. They were cloaked in matching black robes that covered their combat gear and weapons. They were standing near a closed door to a small office of some sort, constantly scanning the crowds, looking for no one in particular.

"Enforcement agents for the controlling family," Jalea explained.

"They always gear up so heavily?"

"Gear up?" Jalea asked, uncertain of her meaning.

"The body armor, the heavy weapons, the commsets," she elaborated. "They look like they're ready for a ground assault."

"Such types prefer to display their strength so as to intimidate potential foes," Jalea said.

"I know the type well," Jessica mumbled. "Are there many of them around?"

"They are usually spread evenly throughout the city."

"Are they like law enforcement or something?" Nathan asked.

"They have no interest in rules," Jalea assured them, "other than the ones involving payment, of course."

"Like I said," Jessica reiterated, "goons." Jessica cast a sidelong glance at them as they passed. "I don't like goons," she said under her breath.

Nathan noticed the type of street vendors was rapidly changing away from prepared foods and goods to bulk produce. There was plenty of pompa root for sale, as well as several other varieties of similar roots. Nathan spied a few odd fruits, various herbs, and even some purple looking vegetables that looked a bit like tomatoes. Of course, there was also plenty of molo at every table. Some of it was pale, some darker, and some of it was already seasoned and dried into what Nathan would forever think of as molo jerky. There was even some that appeared to have been purposefully aged nearly to the point of spoilage, something that, although safe Jalea insisted, was an acquired taste.

"At the end of this street, there should be vendors that deal in the quantities we require," Jalea explained. "Most of the vendors here have traveled in from far out in the country to sell limited amounts of their small harvests in order to purchase things that they cannot produce themselves. We need to find a local grower who lives not too distant and can deliver large quantities."

"What do you think we should buy?" Nathan asked.

"Plenty of molo, of course, and as much as we can, I would expect."

"Why?" Jessica objected.

"Despite its rather unusual flavor, it is quite nutritious. Many people exist on diets that are ninety percent molo."

"If you call that existing," Jessica protested, shuddering at the thought of eating nothing but the odd, slimy fungus.

As Nathan and Jalea continued their stroll, Jessica stopped, pretending to inspect a bundle of herbs, picking it up and sniffing it as she glanced back at the two goons she had spotted earlier. Satisfied the two men had not taken an interest in them, she continued on her way.

She caught up to Nathan and Jalea a few moments later. They had stopped at another vendor table and were looking over the selection of raw molo spread out neatly on the table when Jalea began to speak.

"Good day to you, sir," she offered in a manner that caused Nathan to believe it to be a standard greeting on Haven.

"And good day to you all," the merchant returned. He was an older man, similar in age to their late captain, and had obviously worked outdoors as of late. His hair was pulled back in a short, tight tail, and he wore the clothes of a man who worked the land. There was a manner to him, Nathan noticed, that belied his current trade—something about the way that he moved, the way that he carried himself. He stood tall and proud, unlike the beaten down farmers he had met in Luis's village. "Are you interested in some molo today?" the farmer asked.

"Possibly," Jalea said, "if it is fresh and of a fair price."

"Harvested daily," he boasted. He picked up a piece of the fungus and tore off a corner, handing it to Jalea to inspect.

She held it up to her nose, drawing a sniff in gently to inspect the aroma. She bit off a small piece to taste. "Perhaps too soon." she commented. "It's still bitter."

"It will finish aging in another day," he insisted, "then it will be perfect."

"Of course." Jalea looked about the table, noticing that there were very few varieties available. "Do you mostly sell the paler varieties?"

"I usually have some of the darker varieties, but most of my stock was purchased earlier today. I will have more tomorrow, after today's harvest is concluded."

"Then you live nearby?"

"Not far," he said. "Are you looking to buy in quantity?"

"Yes. An unfortunate accident has left us with a large and hungry crew to feed. We might also be in the market for other types of produce as well."

"How many mouths must you feed?" he asked.

"Maybe fifty for a few weeks at the most."

A puzzled look came across the farmer's face for a moment. "I believe I can supply you with what you need," he promised. "If you like, you may travel with me back to my farm after the market closes. Then you may see for yourself what my humble enterprise has to offer."

"A most gracious offer, sir. I shall consult with my colleagues. Perhaps we shall see you at the day's end."

"I look forward to it," he replied graciously, as they turned and walked away.

\* \* \*

Tobin's vehicle pulled to a stop near his ship in its berth at the spaceport. As Mendez and Weatherly dismounted, another vehicle arrived, delivering four unkempt men.

"Who are they?" Mendez asked Tobin, his hand sliding inside of his cloak to find the butt of his weapon. Tobin gestured for Mendez to remain calm, as the four men approached.

"May I help you?" Tobin asked the leader of the group.

"We're members of the harvesting team you hired," the apparent leader of the group announced. He handed over a small ID card to Tobin for inspection.

"We had expected a single representative," Tobin stated, taking the man's credentials.

"We hoped to ride up with you. It's a bit cramped

in the other ships."

Tobin inspected the man's credentials. Satisfied that they were legitimate, he returned them. "Of course. There is just enough room for the four of you. You may board now. We will depart shortly."

The four new arrivals made their way past and boarded Tobin's ship. Mendez watched as Tobin made arrangements with the ground crew in preparation for departure. After a few minutes, Tobin returned. "Shall we depart?" he asked as he climbed aboard. Sergeant Weatherly followed him in, and after one last look around, Ensign Mendez became the last to climb aboard.

The ship's hatch closed automatically as its engines began to spin up to full power. The ship began to roll slowly out of its berth and onto the taxiway, turning left as it exited its berth.

Mendez looked at the men sharing the small cabin with himself and Sergeant Weatherly. The four of them were dirty, with unwashed hair and worn clothing, and were somewhat lacking in dental hygiene. The leader of the four was staring at Sergeant Weatherly in a menacing fashion. At first, the sergeant chose to ignore the man. But by the time they reached the launch pad and began to rise up off the deck to begin their flight back to the Aurora, he had endured enough.

"Can I help you, old man?" Sergeant Weatherly challenged.

"You look like a soldier," the old man stated with suspicion, as he looked him up and down. "The only soldiers I know are the Takar." The old man looked Weatherly and Mendez over before continuing. "Are you Takar?" he asked, a trace of hatred in his voice.

Sergeant Weatherly could tell that the old man

was trying to bait him. "No," he answered without missing a beat, "but I'm pretty sure I've killed a few," he added, a smile creeping onto his face.

The old man squinted at Sergeant Weatherly for several seconds, a grin finally breaking through his stern gaze. He laughed openly, spitting onto the deck. "I like you."

"Well, that just makes my day, it does," the sergeant answered.

The ship continued to rise in altitude as it streaked away from the spaceport. As it continued to accelerate, the turbulence became more severe. It wasn't as bad as it had been during their descent, but it was still a pretty rough ride. Mendez looked out the window nearest him and saw three ships forming up on their starboard side. Two of them appeared to be small cargo shuttles, while the third one was equipped with some sort of an open scoop under its belly.

"Who the hell are they?" Mendez asked no one in particular.

"Relax. Them's ours," the old man informed him, a puzzled look on his face. "First time in the rings, boy?"

"You might say that," Mendez admitted. "What's that little ship for?"

"That's the harvester," the old man explained. "Scoops up rock and ice from the rings and brings it in to be processed."

Mendez watched as the little ship danced about the others, bobbing in between them and maneuvering around from one side to the other. "What's wrong with that guy?"

"Oh, that's just Josh showing off again. That boy couldn't fly a straight line if his life depended on it!"

The nose on the ship began to pitch up, as her engines began to scream louder, accelerating up and out of the little moon's thick atmosphere. A few moments later, the shaking began to subside as the air thinned and they entered the blackness of space once more.

\* \* \*

The five of them continued to stroll down the crowded street, weaving in and out of the surging crowds as they made their way past the produce merchants. Nathan felt more than one person's glance linger on their group a little longer than he thought normal, which made him a bit apprehensive.

"I get the feeling we kind of stick out in the crowd," he whispered to Jalea.

"No more than any other visitor to Haven," she insisted. "Most of the shoppers are residents of this world. It is rare that an off-worlder shops the street markets here. Most of them don't even come to the surface. They just hire through proxy."

"I would think a crew would want to leave their ship, even if only for a few hours," he offered, "even if just to stretch their legs and get some fresh air."

"Some do, but most would not consider the air of Haven to be *fresh.*" Jalea smiled.

"Yeah, I'd have to agree with them on that point," Jessica said from behind. "Does it always smell like a fungus factory around here?"

"Ah yes, the molo. It is pungent, especially during the harvest."

"Captain, I vote next time we *don't* come during the harvest," Jessica said.

"I'll make a note of it," he promised. "Why is this

molo so popular?"

"It is one of the few plants that continues to grow during the long darkness. The molo does quite nicely in the long, damp nights."

"That explains all the greenhouses we saw on the way in," Nathan added, stopping to examine an odd-looking piece of fruit on one of the vendor's display tables.

"Yes. Most other food is grown in such facilities," Jalea admitted. She picked up the fruit and pulled it apart, offering a piece to each of them to taste. "It is more difficult and requires considerable energy. That makes it more expensive to purchase as well. This is why the people here eat so much molo. It is cheaper. Most of the food grown in the greenhouses is sold to the ships that ply the rings. It is one of the many reasons this world will never fully develop. Had it not been for the riches of the rings, this moon would never have been reformed."

"What do you mean by reformed?" Nathan asked as he chewed his small sample of the strange, purple fruit. It was slightly bitter, with just a touch of sweetness to it. It reminded him of a grape, but with a really chewy texture.

"Haven was not always capable of sustaining life," Jalea explained. "The atmosphere was too thin, and the composition of gases was not correct."

"This world, it was terraformed?" Vladimir asked, a bit of excitement in his voice.

"I am not familiar with this word," Jalea apologized as she indicated to the vendor that she wished to purchase a few pieces of the purple fruit.

"It means *to make Earth-like*," Nathan explained.

"I have never been to Earth," Jalea said, "but I believe the term is correct in this case." She pulled out a few credit chips and paid the vendor for the pieces of fruit.

"It was tried on a few fringe worlds long ago, but we do not know if it was successful," Vladimir added as he ate one of the pieces of fruit.

"I know of several worlds that have been created in this way, and with great success," Jalea assured them. "However, Haven was not one of those successes."

"How so?" Nathan asked. "It seems pretty successful to me."

"It is true; it *is* habitable. Since that was the original goal, then in that sense it was a successful reformation. But because of the long nights, it can support only the most meager of existences, without the aid of substantial infrastructure. As you know, such infrastructure is expensive."

"Then why reform it in the first place?" Jessica asked.

"I suppose they thought it was cheaper in the long run than operating an orbital facility. But of this, I cannot be certain."

"That doesn't make any sense," Nathan commented.

"As I said, I cannot be certain. Nevertheless, the stigma attached to Haven has made it an undesirable destination for most people. As you have probably surmised, it seems to collect the least favorable residents."

"What do you mean... least favorable?" Nathan asked.

"Let's just say that no one comes to Haven by choice, as much as they do by necessity. And if they do come by choice, it is for a very compelling reason."

* * *

Ensign Kaylah Yosef sat at her console on the bridge. Although originally a science officer, she had been serving as the sensor officer ever since they lost more than half of their skeleton crew during the events of their first few jumps. Since then she had been working eighteen-hour days, leaving her station only for trips to the head. After nearly a week of staring at mind-numbing sensor displays, she longed to perform a task that was even slightly *science* related.

As usual, she was watching the various plots of the countless ships flying about the Haven system. Most of them were small ships, cargo shuttles she assumed, that traveled to and fro between the host ships and Haven. The only reason for monitoring all of the traffic was to alert the commander when one of them appeared to be *of interest* and warranted a transfer to the tactical station for more precise tracking.

Whenever something on her display moved, she would check its calculated trajectory to see if it would pass near them. As a small group of ships suddenly changed course, the course projections appeared, indicating they were on an intercept course with the Aurora.

Kaylah straightened up in her seat. "Commander, I've got four ships on an intercept trajectory with us."

"Where are they coming from?" Cameron asked as she stepped up next to Ensign Yosef's console.

"They came from Haven, sir." Kaylah touched the slowly moving icon on the screen that indicated the lead ship in the approaching formation. In a smaller window to the right of the main tracking window, a monochrome line drawing of the selected ship appeared, with all the information the system had to offer on the vessel listed neatly below the image. "One of them matches the profile of Tobin's ship."

"Is there any way to be certain?" Tobin's ship was undoubtedly not the only one of its kind in the area, she surmised.

"No, sir, other than his transponder codes."

"Yeah. And according to ours, we're the Volander," Cameron reminded her.

"Would you like me to hail them, sir?" the communications officer asked.

"In what? Angla? What if it's not them?" Cameron thought for a moment, admonishing herself for discussing her options so openly with the crew. She was sure that Captain Roberts would not have done so. "Any idea what the other ships are?"

Kaylah touched each icon in the formation, calling up line drawings and what little information the ship's sensors could offer. "Well, they're not combatants, that's for sure," Ensign Yosef said, breathing a sigh of relief. "If I had to guess, I'd say they're cargo shuttles of some sort."

"Commander," the communications officer called, "I'm getting a message on one of our tactical comm channels. The ID code belongs to Ensign Mendez."

"Put him on," Cameron ordered, feeling somewhat relieved.

*"Volander, this is Mendez."*

"Go ahead, Ensign," Cameron said.

*"Sergeant Weatherly and I are on Tobin's ship. We're inbound to you, escorting three ships that will be used for the harvesting operations. According*

*to Tobin, our ship and the two larger shuttles will be landing in the hangar bay while the smaller one begins the harvesting operation."*

"Where's the captain?" Cameron asked.

*"He's still on the surface, sir, shopping with the rest of the landing party."*

"Shopping?"

*"Yes, sir. Ensign Nash asked me to secure the hangar deck during the harvesting op in her absence."*

"Understood. Contact me when you're back on board, Ensign. You can fill me in on the *shopping* part."

*"Yes, sir. Mendez out."*

"This ought to be interesting," Cameron decided.


"That ain't no Volonese ship," the old man mumbled.

"Sure she is," Ensign Mendez tried to play off.

"Volonese ships look like a bunch of boxes all tied together," the old man argued. "That there ship is too pretty to be Volonese."

Mendez said nothing, figuring he wasn't going to be able to convince the man otherwise.

"Looks like she's been in a fight as well," he added. He looked sideways at Mendez. "Don't worry, boy. Ain't no Takar-lovers on Haven, that's for sure. Your secrets are safe with us."


A few minutes later, three of the four ships were rolling into the Aurora's hangar bay. The hatch on Tobin's ship, which was the first one into the bay, was deploying as the ship rolled to a stop off to one side at the aft end of the bay.

"You don't want to go any deeper into the bay?" Mendez asked Tobin as he rose from his seat.

"I will be returning to Haven directly," Tobin offered. "I do not want to leave the others without transportation any longer than necessary."

"Sounds good," Mendez said as he headed out of the hatch.

The other two cargo shuttles had already pulled to a stop about halfway into the massive hangar bay and were dropping open their large, rear cargo doors. They were not very attractive ships, basically boxes with four swivel-mounted engines, one on each corner, with a flight deck that looked like half an egg stuck onto the front.

As soon as their big door-ramps hit the deck, they started rolling out large carts, followed by some type of processing apparatus. At least ten workers poured out of each of the two cargo shuttles. The workers, both men and women, did not appear as healthy as the four that had ridden with them in Tobin's ship. Their faces were sullen and devoid of hope, their manner deliberate and paced.

"We're gonna need power for the processors," the old man that had sat next to Mendez in Tobin's ship told him.

"Who are these people?" Mendez asked.

"Just workers," the old man told him as he headed toward the cargo shuttles. Mendez watched as the old man and his companions began hollering orders at the disheveled groups of workers disembarking from the cargo ships. Some of the workers cringed and flinched in fear of the old man and his cohorts.

"Something tells me this ain't right," Mendez said to Sergeant Weatherly. The sergeant simply nodded his agreement. "Keep an eye on things here. I'm gonna round up a few more people to help you out. None of them leaves the hangar bay, understood?"

"Yes, sir," the sergeant answered.

* * *

Vladimir and Danik were busy rummaging through various used parts on a vendor's table. They had been browsing the parts dealers on the back side of the spaceport for more than an hour, and as best as Nathan could tell, Vladimir had not found anything of interest.

"Why don't the Takarans come here?" Nathan asked Jalea.

"The resources harvested from the rings are important to many systems, including some in Takar space. Disruption of the operations here would likely result in unwanted economic repercussions within their own domain," Jalea explained.

"And because the Takarans don't come here, everyone looking to hide from them do," Jessica surmised.

"Yes, but safety is not guaranteed on Haven," Jalea warned. "As you can well imagine, spies are everywhere. I have no doubt that the Takar have operatives here. It would be foolish to assume otherwise."

"How does the controlling family of Haven feel about that?" Nathan asked.

"I doubt they care," Jalea assured him, "as long as their activity does not interfere with business."

"And by business, you mean the collection of fees," Nathan said.

"You learn quickly, Nathan," Jalea complimented.

"Not really. Our history is full of similar examples."

"Ah, yes. We have a saying: 'Times change, but the human animal does not.'"

Vladimir came walking up to them, dusting off his hands as he approached. "I can find nothing here of use. Maybe, if I had more time, and I knew what most of this stuff was, I might find something. I am sorry, my friend."

"No matter," Nathan assured him.

"It is probably best that we head back to the produce area," Jalea told them. "The gentleman we spoke with earlier will be packing up and leaving soon."

\* \* \*

"The last message I got from Ensign Nash was that they were planning to meet with some local farmer later in the day," Ensign Mendez reported to Cameron on the bridge. "They were planning to travel out to some guy's farm to secure a large order of something called molo."

Cameron's face withdrew slightly and the unknown word. "Molo?"

"Some kind of fungus or something. Jess—I mean, Ensign Nash—says it's a cross between a mushroom and tofu," Mendez chuckled. "I got the impression she didn't care for it."

"Doesn't sound too appetizing, does it?" Cameron agreed.

"Anyway, the stuff grows like crazy. We saw whole sheets of it covering hundreds of square meters when we flew in. Tobin says it's very nutritious, although kind of bland. He says you can do a lot with it, though. Apparently it's the mainstay of their diet on Haven."

Cameron was not happy that the rest of the landing party was still on the surface. With Ensign Mendez and Sergeant Weatherly back on the ship, the landing party's security element was now reduced by half. She knew that Jessica was well-trained, and she had proven her abilities in combat twice in the last week. Cameron, however, had expected the trip to last only a few hours, and now it looked like they would be on the surface considerably longer than that.

"Did they say when they would be checking in again?"

"They plan to make contact when they get out to the guy's farm. Ensign Nash doesn't want to use the tight beam array out in the open—too conspicuous and all that. Out on the farm, they can use it without attracting attention."

"Very well," Cameron said, the displeasure still evident on her face.

"If there's nothing else, sir? I should get back to the hangar deck."

"That's all. Thank you, Ensign."

Mendez straightened up and nodded once, before turning to exit.

Although she managed to hide her displeasure from the crew, Cameron was not comfortable with their captain and their chief engineer stuck on an alien world. As far as she was concerned, they were relying far too much on hastily made alliances. Cameron had never been comfortable relying on others, especially strangers.

"Commander," Ensign Yosef hailed, "take a look at this guy. He's a maniac."

Cameron stepped back to Ensign Yosef's station and bent down to get a closer look at the sensor display. At first glance, it seemed like a normal-looking track of the small harvester ship that had been hired by Tobin. But as the numbers continued to update, she realized what the ensign was talking about. "Has he been flying like that the whole time?" Cameron asked.

"Yeah. At first I thought the sensors where out of calibration, but I checked. Those numbers are accurate."

Cameron watched as the small ship weaved its way around the larger components in the rings while scooping up the smaller ones. "He barely slows down when he scoops them up," she declared, a bit surprised. "Can you generate a real-time 3D model of this?"

"No, sir. We're still down more than half of our cores," she apologized. "I could compile it later into a playback, if you'd like."

"No thanks," Cameron said. "Just thought it would be interesting to watch." She watched a few more seconds, still shocked by the abrupt maneuvering of the harvester. "Whoever is flying that thing really knows what they're doing; I'll give him that."

# CHAPTER FOUR

By the time Nathan and the others had returned from the parts market, most of the raw produce vendors had already packed up for the day.

"You have returned," the farmer called to them as they approached. He had completely disassembled his tables and canopy and was finishing loading them onto his vehicle. "Does this mean you are still interested in purchasing some molo?"

"Indeed it does," Jalea answered. "Does your invitation still stand?"

"Indeed it does," the farmer smiled back to her. "I sold well today, so there is plenty of room for you all."

"How will we get back?" Jessica whispered to Nathan and Jalea.

"We can contact Tobin. The farms are outside of the city, so there are no restrictions on landing. He can pick us up at any time," Jalea assured them.

The farmer tossed the last crate up onto his flatbed hauler, dusted off his hands, and returned to them. "My name is Redmon Tugwell," he announced, extending his hand. "My friends simply call me Tug."

"Then we should call you..." Nathan began, taking his hand.

"If you're going to buy a bunch of my molo, then I guess you should call me Tug as well."

"Okay, Tug. Nice to meet you. I'm Nathan. This

is Jalea, Jessica, and those two back there are Vladimir and Danik."

"It's a pleasure to meet you all. If everyone will climb on board, we can get started. It'll take about an hour to get there."

The vehicle was basically one big platform with wheels. At the front of the vehicle, the center portion was raised, covering the main drive section of the vehicle, behind which was a bench seat with room on either side of the driver for passengers. In the middle of the raised section was a small control console, with a steering column and a dash-mounted throttle to one side. On the opposite side of the console there was a small handbrake lever. There were rails along both sides of the platform, with fold-down benches built into the rails. The side rails appeared easily removable, giving the flatbed vehicle the ability to haul objects considerably larger than the bed itself.

Tug climbed aboard first, reaching behind him to fold down the most forward bench seat on each side. "Everyone grab a seat and we'll be on our way," he instructed as he positioned himself behind the driver's console in the middle of the front bench seat.

Tug held out his hand, pulling Jalea up to sit beside him on his right. Nathan took a seat on Tug's left, with Jessica sitting directly behind him, and Vladimir and Danik on the opposite bench.

"Hang on," Tug announced. "It's not exactly a smooth ride."

Tug pushed the throttle forward slowly, causing the vehicle to lurch forward. The vehicle itself was quiet, the wheels creating the only perceptible sound as the dirt and gravel crunched beneath them.

They rolled down the back roads at a slow

and steady rate, stopping occasionally to yield to other vehicles or pedestrians. The streets were less congested than they had been earlier in the day when they had first arrived, therefore their rate of travel was considerably better. Tug explained that the city was most active in the morning and early afternoon, and that by this time most merchants had already begun to make their way home for the day. The days were a few hours longer on Haven than on Earth, so most people spent the first half of the day conducting business in town, and the second half at their homes, most of which were small farms.

Nathan was surprised at how few people actually lived in the city proper. Other than merchants that lived above their shops, and a few small communities that housed mostly ring workers and technicians working the spaceport, nearly everyone else that lived on Haven resided on small parcels of land spread throughout the surrounding countryside. It entailed daily commuting into the city, but with the extra hours available each day, it did not seem to be a hindrance.

After about ten minutes, they found themselves on the outskirts of the city, moving at a much better speed as they made their way through the countryside.

The land was mostly flat with only modest rises in elevation from time to time. The road was dotted with farmhouses both large and small. Nearly all of them had at least one greenhouse; many had several and of various sizes. There was also molo growing everywhere—along the road, between rows of greenhouses. Anywhere you would expect to see lawns, there was molo. Nathan had to wonder why they needed to travel farther out in the country to purchase molo from this guy when there was so much of it growing all around them.

Nathan noticed that where the land was open and exposed, it seemed dried out. He could easily see how little would thrive naturally on this reformed world.

"Why is it so dry?" he asked Tug.

"There is no rain on Haven," Tug explained. "Not any real weather of any kind, actually."

"But you do have some natural vegetation in addition to the molo, so there must be some water."

"There is ground water, yes. And as you have probably noticed, the air here is pretty humid as well."

"Yeah, I got that."

"When we go through our dark cycle, the temperature drops, and most of the humidity in the atmosphere settles back down onto the land. When the light returns, for the first few weeks everything becomes green on Haven."

"So I'm guessing it's not long until the darkness starts?" Jessica surmised.

"That's right," Tug told her. "In four days the long night will begin."

"And it really lasts fifty-two days?" Nathan asked.

"What do you do all that time?" Jessica wondered. "Doesn't it get cold?"

"Very. We stay inside, mostly. I work the greenhouses, where it is warm. But there is very little activity during this time, at least out in the country."

"Sounds like a typical Russian winter," Vladimir exclaimed.

"It is not as bad in the city," Tug went on as they continued to bounce down the road. "They have a lot of lighting and heaters to keep the cold away."

"That must be those vents we saw on the sides of the buildings."

"Yes, they blow warm air out into the street. It is wasteful, but necessary. There were plans to enclose much of the city in a dome, but it is doubtful that they will spend the time and money to do so."

"Sounds rough to me," Jessica said.

"You don't like the cold?" Vladimir asked.

"I grew up in Florida," she explained. "We don't do cold there."

"Where I grew up, we had snow and ice for at least half of the year. Very cold," Vladimir said. "But when the snow would melt, everything was green and beautiful."

"Well, it never gets *beautiful* on Haven. It isn't pretty, but it *is* out of the way and we *are* left alone. And because of the rings, we can get what we need out here."

Nathan continued to gaze at the stark landscape as they traveled. "You know, there isn't any wildlife here," he stated. "I just realized—I haven't seen so much as a bird, a squirrel, or even a dog the entire time we've been here. Don't you have any animals on Haven?"

"There are some," Tug assured him. "None that are indigenous to this world, as it was a lifeless rock before it was reformed."

"Not even pets?" Nathan wondered.

"A few, but most people cannot afford such luxuries."

"Surely you have livestock of some type?" Nathan asked. "You know: cows, chickens, pigs, goats. Animals you can eat?"

"Yes, of course. But again, such creatures are

expensive to acquire and to care for. They are rare on Haven and only for the rich. Those that own such keep them indoors, to protect against the cold as well as theft."

"There are bugs," Jessica commented, as she swatted something that had landed on her neck.

"Yes," Tug laughed. "Somehow, they always manage to find their way onto every human inhabited world."

\* \* \*

"He's coming in awfully fast," Ensign Yosef warned. By now, news of the harvester pilot's skills had spread, and there were a few more people on the bridge than usual, all wanting to witness his first landing.

"Put up the flight deck approach camera," Cameron ordered. On the main view screen, the image switched from the standard view ahead to one facing aft toward the open flight deck between the center of the ship and the massive drive section at her stern. A small point on the screen, nothing more than a glint of reflected light, was dropping toward them, growing larger as it descended.

"He's coming in high as well," Cameron noted.

Within moments the speck blossomed into the ungainly shape of the harvester. It came in low, skimming quickly over the tail of the ship. No sooner had it cleared the drive section than it dropped further, pulled its nose up, and flared its landing thrusters to decelerate sharply.

"*Volander, Harvester,*" the pilot's voice came over the comm channel. "*You might wanna open your outer bay door so I don't roll right into it.*"

"Open it," Cameron ordered.

The outer transfer bay door began lifting open as the harvester finished its flaring maneuver, settling onto the deck with enough forward momentum left to roll into the primary airlock bay. Without hesitation, the small harvester rolled under the rising airlock door, barely clearing, and then slammed on its brakes to stop just as it was about to kiss the inner door.

*"Volander, Harvester. We're in, close her up."*

The airlock bay door immediately began to slide back down as the harvester powered down her main engines in preparation to enter the hangar bay.

"Damn. Was that really necessary?" Cameron asked. Although his skills were impressive, she wasn't too pleased with his reckless landing on *her* ship.

"Probably not," Ensign Yosef agreed, "but it was impressive."

"You have the conn, Ensign. I'm going to have a little chat with that hotshot about proper landing procedures." Without waiting for a response, Cameron turned and headed out of the bridge.

The harvester rolled into the hangar bay, turning sharply to port before stopping. As it came to a complete stop, one of the ground crew ran underneath and opened up a control panel along the harvester's undercarriage. After manipulating the controls, several locking mechanisms disengaged and the entire collection pod dropped smoothly off the bottom of the harvester and onto the deck. Moments later, two more workers were rolling the massive pod away to be unloaded. Meanwhile, others were connecting a refueling line that came from one of their nearby cargo shuttles.

Cameron came charging into the bay, marching up to Ensign Mendez, who was overseeing the security of the operation.

"Ensign Mendez," she snapped. "I want to have a word with that pilot," she ordered, pointing toward the cockpit of the harvester.

"Uh, yes, sir. But I think you'll have to talk to their crew foreman, sir," Mendez answered.

"And who would that be?"

"That would be me, lady." The old man that had challenged Mendez back on Tobin's shuttle stepped over from where he had been overseeing the manual offload of the harvester's collection pod.

"Commander," Mendez started, "this is the foreman."

"Marcus Wallace, at your service, ma'am."

"Mister Wallace, I'd like a word with one of your pilots," Cameron insisted in no uncertain terms.

"I'm assuming you mean Josh."

"If he's the reckless jerk flying that harvester, then yes." Cameron looked over at the cockpit windows of the harvester. She could see the helmeted pilot as he checked his systems in preparation for departure. His face was obscured by the reflection on his faceplate, but he saw Cameron looking his way and gave her a little mock salute. For a moment, she could've sworn she saw a smirk on his face.

"I'm afraid that won't be possible, ma'am. You see, he's in the middle of a hot refuel, so he can't leave the cockpit. Besides, he'll be taking off again shortly."

"Well you tell that little hotshot that he needs to call in for approach and follow the controller's guidelines. Because the next time he comes in to my flight deck like a bat outta hell, he's going to find himself slamming headlong into the outer bay door. Is that understood?"

"Yes, ma'am," Marcus chuckled.

Ensign Mendez started to smile, then stopped when his eyes met his commander's as she turned and charged out of the bay.

Marcus lowered his headset mic. "Joshua, I trust you copied all of that."

*"I gotta ask nicely next time?"* Josh joked over the comm.

"If you don't mind. And maybe you can ease up on the throttle as well."

*"Okay, but that's gonna take all the fun out of it."*

"All right!" Marcus hollered. "Let's get that pod unloaded, get it strapped back on, and get him the hell outta here! MOVE IT, PEOPLE!"

Workers scrambled to remove the last of the rubble from the collection pod before rolling it back under the harvester. With a touch of the controls, the pod raised up until it mated with the underside of the harvester, its latches grasping tightly and its wheels retracting up into her undersides. A warning klaxon sounded once from the harvester and its motion warning lights began to flash, warning everyone on the deck that it was about to start moving. A few seconds later, the harvester backed up slightly, pivoted its nose aft, and started rolling out of the hangar bay and back into the transfer airlock.

*"Volander, Harvester. Requesting permission for departure,"* Josh's voice crackled over the comms.

Marcus smiled. "Good boy."

\* \* \*

As they got farther away from the city, the farms became more spread out, with greater amounts of undeveloped space between them. Eventually, they turned off on a small side road that led into a canyon of sorts. It was about a hundred meters long and forty meters across, and it looked like a large trench.

"What is this place?" Nathan asked.

"Home," Tug laughed.

"No, I mean how did it get this way?"

"As best I can tell, it's a large sinkhole."

"You're kidding."

"There are quite a few of them scattered all over this moon," Tug told him. "Most people think it has something to do with the way this moon was reformed. In order to thicken the atmosphere, they pulled a lot of moisture out of subsurface aquifers, many of which were originally frozen. A few people have even put a roof over the smaller ones and created their own little habitats inside. Mine is a bit large for that."

They drove down into the sinkhole along a road cut into one side. There were long greenhouses built along each side, with small storage buildings in between each one. As they made their way through the middle of the compound, they could see stacks of molo, all cut and bailed, ready to be sold at market.

"Is that all molo?" Nathan asked.

"Yes. Fate smiled on us both this day. This was

all due to be delivered to another buyer, but they backed out at the last moment. Had you not come along, I would've had to prep and dehydrate all of this in order to preserve it. To avoid all of that extra work, I am willing to give you an excellent deal on this batch."

"Where did you grow all of this?"

"Here, before the harvest, the molo covered the ground from wall to wall. The bottom of this sinkhole has a higher moisture content than the ground above. The molo grows denser and more quickly here than in most places."

"How long does it take to grow?"

"Only a few weeks."

"Damn," Jessica exclaimed. "It's a fungus factory."

The vehicle pulled to the far end of the sinkhole, coming to a stop in front of a large building situated in the middle of the back wall. The building, which Nathan assumed was the main residence, was connected to another building directly behind it, which in turn was connected via tunnels on either side to the rows of greenhouses wrapping around the compound. From the looks of the layout, Nathan figured the residents could probably go the entire dark season without ever going outside.

"This is it," Tug announced as the vehicle stopped.

As they climbed down, a young girl and a woman several years younger than Tug came out of the main house to greet them. The woman looked wary of the strangers, the young girl only curious. The woman squinted, trying to see the faces of the strangers that had come home with her husband.

"It's okay, Ranni. These people have come to buy our molo."

Jessica's hand immediately moved inside her cloak to grab her sidearm, as light reflected off something along side of the woman.

Nathan noticed Jessica's reaction. "What is it?" he whispered.

"She's armed."

"Wait," Nathan warned. "Maybe she's just being cautious."

Nathan watched as Tug approached his wife, followed by Jalea. After a few steps, both of them came out of the amber glare of the low afternoon sun and into the cleaner illumination cast by the house lights, making her better able to see their faces. The woman suddenly began to relax, laying a large energy weapon against the wall behind her as her daughter left her side and ran to her approaching father. Jessica's hand eased off her hidden sidearm, withdrawing her empty hand from her cloak.

"Papa!" the girl squealed as she jumped into his outstretched arms. He scooped her up and hugged her, kissing her cheek repeatedly. "What did you bring me, Papa?"

He set her back down and reached into his pocket, pulling out a small piece of candy. "Your favorite," he said, handing her the candy.

"Thank you, Papa," the little girl said as she took the candy.

"Now go back inside, sweetie. Papa still has work to do." Tug turned back to Nathan and the others. "If you would like to inspect the molo, to determine if it is to your liking, I will rejoin you shortly." Tug bowed slightly as he turned to follow his wife inside.

"Thanks for not shooting her, Jess," Nathan said.

"Good she didn't raise that thing," Jessica replied. "I would've dropped her without a thought."

"I do not believe these people pose any threat to you," Jalea scolded.

"I'm sure you're right," Nathan answered. "Shall we inspect the molo?" he asked, gesturing for Jalea to lead the way.

Jalea walked past them toward the stacks of bailed molo, casting a disapproving gaze toward Jessica as she and Nathan turned to follow.

"Yeah, let's go look at the pretty mushrooms," Jessica mumbled as she passed.

"Some fun, eh, my friend?" Vladimir mused.

As they walked away, Nathan could hear an argument arising between Tug and his wife from inside the house. They were using their native tongue, so Nathan couldn't understand them. But he was pretty sure that Tug's wife was not happy about her husband's surprise guests. A quick glance at Vladimir told Nathan his friend had come to the same conclusion.

\* \* \*

Tobin sat down at his usual table in the small cafe near Haven spaceport. Having just returned from delivering the work crew to the Aurora, it was his first opportunity to partake in more familiar cuisine. As he began his meal, a nefarious looking man sat down at the table behind him, his back facing Tobin's.

"I trust our guests have arrived." The stranger sitting behind him spoke softly, as if to himself, barely loud enough for Tobin to hear over the noise of the cafe.

"They have," Tobin responded between bites. "And my payment?"

"Already in your account."

Tobin pulled a mini data pad out of his pocket and checked his account balance, the sum of which drew a smile on his face. "Excellent," he mumbled to himself as he placed the pad on the table and continued his meal.

"It was a large sum to provide on such short notice. You're lucky we have assets in the system," the man said.

"Please," Tobin scoffed, "do not insult me with your lies."

"We grow impatient, Tobin. What is their location?"

"Patience. You will know soon enough."

"I will know now, worm," the man insisted, his still low voice taking a threatening tone.

"They are not currently accessible," Tobin lied. The truth was he hadn't spoken with them in several hours and did not in fact know their current whereabouts.

"Stick to the plan, my friend. Just be at my berth with your people at the proper time."

The man grumbled. "You'd better be right about this one, Tobin." The man finished his drink in one long gulp and departed without saying another word. Tobin continued eating his meal, an almost giddy look of anticipation of things to come on his face.

\* \* \*

"I trust the molo meets with your approval." Tug asked as he approached.

"Yes, I'm sure it will be fine," Nathan said.

"How much are you asking?" It was obvious that

Jalea did not think it wise for Nathan to do the negotiating.

"I'd say ten standard credits per kilogram is a fair price."

"And there are fifty kilos per bail?" Jalea asked.

"That is correct. You can have all twenty bails, if you like."

Jalea turned to Nathan. "It is a fair deal. I doubt you will find better."

"How much should we buy?" Nathan had no idea how many meals that amount of molo would provide for his crew. Nor did he have any idea how much revenue their harvesting operation would bring. He was forced to place his trust in Jalea's understanding of the matter.

"I see no reason not to purchase the entire amount. If preserved properly, it should last you and your crew several weeks, if not longer."

"And we can afford it?" he added in a whisper.

Jalea nodded slightly, as she turned back to Tug. "We will take the entire amount. That would be ten thousand credits, correct?"

"That is correct. How are you to make payment?"

"We are currently engaged in harvesting operations in the ring. Once we sell some of the harvest in the market tomorrow morning, we will be able to pay you for your molo."

"That will be fine, I'm sure. I will have to hold delivery until payment has been made. I'm sure you understand."

"Of course," Jalea agreed.

"I can deliver it to port, if you wish."

"That will not be necessary," Jalea assured him. "We will have it picked up by shuttle tomorrow."

"If you prefer," Tug agreed. "If you'd like, you're

all welcome to stay for dinner. I can have my wife prepare some of her delicious molo stew. Then you will taste for yourself the quality of the product you are purchasing. And for a few extra credits, I might even be able to convince her to bestow her recipe upon you."

"We are honored by your invitation," Jalea bowed. "Captain, I trust that would be acceptable." Jalea flashed Nathan a look urging him to accept.

"An honor indeed," Nathan stated graciously, trying his best to speak in similar fashion.

"Wonderful," Tug said. "I will inform my wife that we have guests for dinner." Tug bowed his head before heading back to his house.

"Great," Jessica commented. "Mushroom stew down on the farm. And to think, I joined the fleet to get *off* the farm."

"I thought you said you were from Florida." Vladimir commented.

"What, you think Florida is all beaches and bikinis?" Jessica sniped.

"I'm not sure staying for dinner is such a great idea, Jalea," Nathan said. "I'm not sure we should hang around that long."

"Agreed," Jessica added quickly, looking for any opportunity to avoid having to eat more molo.

"It would be quite rude to turn down the invitation, Captain," Jalea warned. "And you did say that you wanted to learn more about this part of space. How did you put it, 'take a look around'? Perhaps this might be such an opportunity."

"Perhaps you're right," Nathan nodded. "Sorry, Jess."

Jessica rolled her eyes. She knew he was right, that it was a good opportunity to gather more intel.

"Dinner hosts are usually chatty," she admitted. Nathan turned back to Jalea. "Contact Tobin and arrange for a pickup later tonight."

"As you wish," she said as she stepped away.

"Jessica, set up the tight beam mini-dish and try to make contact with the Aurora—I mean the Volander. Let them know what's going on."

\* \* \*

Ensign Mendez watched as the workers carried trays of separated ores from the processor to the cargo shuttle. The workers were an odd mixture of different types of people, all men except for three women, all with no noticeable similarities between them. Although they seemed to be moving at a steady, relentless pace, the foreman continued to yell at them incessantly.

To his right, one of the flight crew for the harvesting team sat snacking on some dried substance. "Who are these people?" Mendez asked the flight technician.

"Just workers," he replied.

"What do you mean 'just workers'?"

"They come from all over. Some of them come voluntarily. Others are purchased."

"What? Like slaves?"

"Not slaves, really. They usually owe someone lots of money. They sell themselves into labor contracts in order to pay off their debt."

"And how long are these contracts?"

"It depends on the size of their debt. Usually a few years, at least."

Mendez shook his head as he walked away. He walked casually around the hangar bay, as he had done every so often since the harvesting operations had begun. He didn't do it because it was necessary, but rather to give the appearance of being vigilant as a deterrent to anyone thinking of sneaking off the flight deck. But the workers had proven to be just that—workers. They appeared to have little interest in anything other than surviving their long, grueling shifts, which thus far appeared to be never-ending.

As he made his rounds, he decided to veer off his perimeter walk, instead turning inward and walking along the sorting line. A string of about ten workers stood along either side of a long conveyor belt that moved rubble from the hopper, which had been unloaded from the harvester, to a cargo container at the other end nearer the cargo shuttle. As the rubble passed by, the workers, who wore some type of special scanning eye-wear, picked out certain pieces, depositing them into containers at their sides. When one of the containers became full, another worker would replace it with an empty one and carry the full container off to the processor.

Mendez came to a stop at the far end of the conveyor line, standing next to the old foreman, Marcus. "What are they sorting?"

"They're pickin' out pieces with the highest concentrations of precious metals. You know, gold, silver—hell, there's even diamonds in these rings. Theory is there used to be two stars in this system, but the first one went supernova eons ago. Most of the ring is composed of a massive planet that was blown off of its orbit when the first star blew up, and the planet drifted too close to the gas giant and got pulled apart."

"Don't you have machines that can do the sorting?"

"Sure. But machines cost money. Machines breakdown. Workers are cheaper and more versatile." He smiled, eyeing an attractive, although somewhat disheveled, young female worker on the sorting line.

Just then, one of the workers on the sorting line, a middle-aged man, leaned over on both hands on the edge of the conveyor. He was obviously exhausted, and was simply trying to rest for a moment. Nevertheless, his unauthorized respite quickly earned him the foreman's wrath.

"What the hell do you think you're doing?" Marcus bellowed as he stormed off toward the exhausted worker. "Did you hear anyone call for a break?"

"Hey!" Mendez interrupted, grabbing the foreman's arm to slow his progress. "Ease up! Can't you see he's just tired?"

"I don't give a damn if he's tired! He's paid to work, not rest!"

"I said ease up!" Mendez insisted. This time, his tone made it clear that it wasn't a suggestion.

The foreman turned to confront the ensign, bound and determined not to let anyone tell him how to run his crew. The tired worker did not want to be the cause of the dispute, knowing that even if he avoided punishment now, it would surely come later.

"It's okay," the worker assured Mendez. "I'm okay. I can work." The man straightened back up and started working again. "See, I'm working. I'm sorry, sir."

Marcus turned back to Mendez, staring him cold in the eyes.

"You got something to say?" Mendez asked in a challenging tone.

The foreman looked the young ensign over, taking

special notice of both his close-quarters weapon and his sidearm. The look of confidence in the ensign's eyes told the foreman all he needed to know. This was not a man to be underestimated. With nothing more than a grunt, the foreman returned to his monitoring position at the end of the conveyor line.

# CHAPTER FIVE

"It smells wonderful," Jalea insisted politely.

Tug's wife had brought the food in from the kitchen without so much as a single utterance. Although she had remained politely quiet thus far, it was obvious by the tension between her and Tug that she did not appreciate nor approve of the unexpected dinner guests.

"Ranni is an excellent cook. I apologize if there is not much variety, as we have not yet purchased our stock for the darkness."

"I'm sure it will be more than enough," Jalea told him as she passed the first dish of fried molo around the table.

"It's a very nice place you have here, Tug," Jessica stated, hoping to break the ice. She knew this dinner was the perfect opportunity to collect more intelligence, even if it meant having to force down more molo. "You've done quite well for yourself."

"We've managed, perhaps better than some," he admitted, a bit of pride reflected in his voice. "It's not a bad life. Hard work, yes, but not as hard as those working the rings."

"A lot of people on Haven work the rings?"

"On Haven, there are two career paths," Tug explained. "You either work the rings, or you provide for those that work the rings. That is the sole reason this world was reformed. People come from all over the sector to work the rings of Haven."

"Why is that?" Nathan asked. "I mean, if it's such hard work that is."

"It depends. There are basically two kinds working the rings. Those that came here on their own, and those that had no choice in the matter."

"What do you mean *had no choice*?" Nathan inquired.

"A man can earn a lot of money in a short time working the rings. Those that do—and survive— usually depart with enough wealth to start over someplace nicer. Maybe even start their own business on a more prosperous world. But sadly, most have come to pay off debts."

"What, like contract workers?" Nathan asked.

"Something like that. When someone is unable to pay their debts, they offer themselves up as indentured workers. Their creditor can then sell them to teams here on Haven, as well as several other worlds. These workers then have to complete their contract."

"Sounds more like indentured slaves to me," Jessica commented.

"There are many who would also consider that term to be accurate," Tug agreed. "It may seem barbaric, but it is a system that has been in place for centuries. Unfortunately, it also has made Haven into a popular place for criminals, thugs, and other nefarious types."

"I find it curious that the Takarans don't venture out here," Jessica said, hoping to take the conversation in a direction that would yield more useful information.

"Actually, it's pronounced *Ta'Akar*. It's the proper name of the family that has ruled that part of space for nearly a millennium. They do not bother this system because to do so would bring resistance from many of their neighboring systems. You see, many depend on the resources of these rings. Not all are blessed with such accessible abundance. And many of those that were so blessed have long since depleted them. The Ta'Akar systems do not *need* the resources of Haven, but they find it best not to anger those that do. However, many believe the Ta'Akar do have spies on Haven, although this has never been proven."

"You seem to know quite a bit about the Ta'Akar," Jessica commented, the slightest hint of suspicion in her tone.

"No more than most," Tug assured her.

"So, were you born here?" Jessica asked.

"No. I came here much by accident."

"How so?"

"I was a fighter pilot in the Palee Militia. My ship was damaged in combat and I spent several weeks adrift. I was rescued by a cargo vessel that was headed for Haven. They recovered my ship, expecting a valid salvage. When they found me alive, they had little choice but to allow me passage. But they left me and my ship stranded on Haven. With no way back to Palee, I had little choice but to make Haven my home. So I sold one of the reactors from my ship in order to buy this modest farm."

"What happened to the rest of your ship?" Vladimir asked.

"I scavenged a few systems from it, but it is mostly still intact. It is stored in one of the barns."

"Really?" Vladimir exclaimed. "I would love to take a look at it, if you do not mind, of course."

"Not at all."

"And you've been working as a molo farmer ever since?" Jessica asked.

"For nearly twenty years."

"How did you meet your wife?"

"I spotted her at the labor hall one day. She was on a work crew that I hired to build some greenhouses. I was smitten from the moment I saw her, so I bought out her contract."

Jessica's eyes widened with shock. "You mean you bought a wife?"

"No, I merely freed her from her obligations. I did not force her to stay with me. I even offered to pay for passage back to her world, but she refused to accept charity and insisted on earning the passage by working for me. Eventually, things just happened."

"So she never earned the passage, huh?" Nathan joked.

"Oh, she keeps the money hidden in a box somewhere," Tug laughed. "Sometimes she threatens to use it, when she is most angry with me." Tug scooped up another helping of stew. "But enough about me. What about all of you? Where do you come from? I recognize the accents and mannerisms of these two," Tug stated, pointing at Jalea and Danik. "But the rest of you are quite different. I don't believe I've ever met your kind before."

"They are from a quite distant star," Jalea said.

"Really?" Tug stroked his chin, looking at his guests. "And how is it you find yourself so far from home?"

Jessica cast a displeased look upon Jalea. Prior to their departure from the Aurora, Jessica had counseled Nathan to avoid giving away too much information. Now she wished she had issued the same warning to Jalea.

Nathan chose his answer carefully. "A series of unfortunate events has led us to your world."

"I see. And what is your business here?" Tug was intrigued by this news. He glanced at Jalea, who met his gaze without response.

"We're just looking for a way to return home, as quickly as possible."

"And have you found a way?"

"We're still weighing options at the moment," Nathan told him.

Tug surveyed his guests once more. "There is an old legend. It is one that the Ta'Akar have been trying to suppress for centuries. It tells how we all came from a faraway star. This legend has been the center of a controversy that has lasted countless generations."

"How so?" Nathan asked.

"Several centuries after the Ta'Akar took control of their world, they tried to convince the people that this legend was false, that they had been born of their own world. The people resisted, as the legend had served to support their own religious beliefs for as long as anyone could remember. But the Ta'Akar were persistent in their efforts, eventually resorting to brutality as their primary means of coercion."

"And this worked?" Jessica asked.

"At first, no. But eventually the people grew tired of resistance, and they simply accepted the doctrine. Publicly, all agreed with the Ta'Akar doctrine, but many continued to believe otherwise, in secret."

"And what do you believe?" Nathan asked. "If you don't mind my asking."

"I am not sure what I believe," Tug answered honestly. "However, I do not believe in the Ta'Akar 'Doctrine of Origins.'"

"And this doctrine," Nathan said, "it has lasted all this time?"

"You sound surprised," Tug said.

"It's just that such things generally fade as power changes hands over the generations."

"Yes, but that is not the case with the Ta'Akar," Tug explained. "You see, the royal family is privy to special treatments that greatly prolong their life span. The last ruler was in power for more than two centuries. And the current ruler is expected to be in power even longer."

"Really?" Although the formula for such treatments had been found in the Data Ark on Earth, they had only added a few decades to the human life span, not centuries. And only then by somewhat delaying the onset of aging. "And this doctrine, is this the basis of the rebellion I've heard so much about?" Nathan wasn't sure how Tug would react to his question, but he had a feeling there was more to the farmer than he let on.

"Ah yes, the rebellion." Tug smiled as he regarded Nathan's question. "As you probably know, people do not generally care to be told how to think. Eventually, more and more of the Ta'Akar people began to openly reject the doctrine. When the military tried to force the matter, it sparked a violent backlash that quickly spread throughout all of Ta'Akar space. A rebellion erupted that has been going on for more than two decades. It has cost many lives on both sides, and has cost the Ta'Akar many systems over the years."

"You mean they once controlled more than just the five systems they control now?" Jessica asked.

"Oh yes. The Ta'Akar once controlled twice that number. But the war has forced them to abandon the outer systems in order to maintain control over their core worlds," Tug explained. "In fact, this system was once under Ta'Akar control."

"So they were spread too thin?" Jessica was hoping to get some information about the Ta'Akar forces.

"Yes. They did not expect such heavy resistance at first and were caught unprepared. They lost many ships and had problems with mass defections amongst their forces. Had they not pulled out of the fringe systems, I doubt they would have defeated the rebels at all."

"Then the war is over?" Nathan asked.

"Recently, the Ta'Akar launched an offensive against the last of the rebel forces that were in hiding. Rumor has it that only a small, insignificant number escaped and that the Ta'Akar are claiming victory. I suspect they will continue to hunt survivors down until all have been eliminated."

Nathan noticed a melancholy in Tug's voice. "You seem disappointed."

"If this rumor is true, it is only a matter of time before the Ta'Akar reclaim their lost systems."

"Many believe they will not stop there," Jalea added.

"You think they'll try to expand again," Nathan deduced.

"If the Ta'Akar wish to prevent future civil unrest," Tug explained, "it would be wise for them to expand their domain in order to vastly increase their base of power."

"Make themselves too big to overthrow," Jessica commented.

"But if their forces are weakened, as you say, then wouldn't expansion be difficult?"

"One would think," Tug said. "However, it is believed that the Ta'Akar are close to perfecting a new power source, one that will give them nearly limitless energy. If this is true, there will be no stopping them."

The conversation fell silent on that note. While Nathan was curious about this new power source, he couldn't help but be annoyed by the fact that the information had been yet another fact that Jalea had kept hidden from them.

"What do you know about this power source?" Jessica asked.

"Only that the research is being conducted on the Ta'Akar home world, and that it is said to be nearing completion," Tug said.

"How is it you know so much about it?" Jessica asked. "You would think something like this would be kept secret."

"The Ta'Akar have continued to talk openly of this project. They consider their home system impenetrable. Knowledge of their coming power source serves to keep the restlessness of the Ta'Akar population under control. It gives them hope for a better, more stable future."

The room fell silent once again, as they considered Tug's statements. "But enough of this talk of rebellions and doctrine. It is too depressing for dinner conversation." Tug turned to Vladimir. "We have heard little from you this night, Vladimir. Tell me of your world."

Vladimir looked at Nathan, unsure of what to say. Nathan nodded slightly and shrugged. "Our world is beautiful place," he began, choosing his words carefully. "It has many diverse climates and environments, as well as many different cultures and civilizations, some of which date back thousands of years." Vladimir was proud of his Russian heritage. His culture had been one of the few that had survived the great bio-digital plague without becoming diluted beyond recognition.

"Truly? Your civilization is that old?" Tug was surprised by the revelation. "Then how is it we have never come across your kind before?"

"We've only recently begun venturing out into distant space," Jessica interrupted.

"Then you're explorers?"

"Yes, in a manner of speaking," Nathan admitted.

"But then, aren't we all?" Tug concluded.

Vladimir, who had finished his food quickly as usual, moved to excuse himself. "If nobody has any objections, perhaps I could take a look at your ship while the rest of you continue with your meal."

"Of course," Tug insisted. "The ship is in the large barn at the far end of the compound. Out the front door, and straight ahead. You cannot miss it."

"Thank you," Vladimir said as he rose.

Jalea uttered words to Danik in their language, after which he too rose to join Vladimir.

"Captain," Tug began, "I am curious about something."

The statement instantly raised Jessica's concern. She nudged Nathan's leg with her own as a reminder of caution.

"What might that be?" Nathan asked in his most diplomatic tone.

"This world you come from, your friend says it is thousands of years old. Yet I have never heard of a civilization that was much more than a millennium old, save for one. Could your world be that one?"

Nathan felt backed into a corner. This farmer,

who had not turned out to be as simple as he would have others believe, seemed to have considerable knowledge of the area of the galaxy they happened to be stranded in. Also, he suspected there was far more that the farmer was not telling him that undoubtedly would be useful information.

Being straightforward and direct had always served Nathan well in the past, but the stakes were much higher now, and he quite possibly was out of his element under the current circumstances. "And if it were, what would that mean to you?" Nathan asked, trying to deflect a question with a question.

"That is a complicated question, Captain, with a complicated answer."

"I'll try to keep up," Nathan told him, a slight smile forming at the corner of his mouth. He cast a sidelong glance at Jessica, who didn't seem terribly impressed with his efforts to avoid the topic thus far.

"Perhaps it would be best if I were to explain the legend more clearly," Tug began. "The legend states that all human life began on a single, faraway world called Earth. Nearly thirteen thousand years ago, the people of this world began to venture out to nearby stars. Somehow, along the way, they angered their gods, and as a punishment were infested with a terrible evil that quickly spread throughout all their worlds. Many fled, seeking to escape the evil before they too were consumed by its horrors. Some groups managed to escape untainted and start anew on untouched worlds, while others were already infiltrated by those touched by evil. Such worlds fell even before they had started, causing some of their people to flee even farther out into the galaxy."

"And this is one of those systems?" Nathan asked.

"In a manner," Tug explained. "It is believed that several of these ships eventually settled in the Pentaurus cluster. Its five stars made possible an interstellar civilization that developed rapidly due to an abundance of resources and numerous habitable worlds. Being in such close proximity to one another enabled the settlements to share the technology and resources they had brought with them in a way that benefited all, at least at first." Tug picked up the bottle of drink and distributed the remainder of its contents equally amongst their glasses as he continued speaking. "Until one world decided they wanted more, and that the best way to get it was by force."

"The Ta'Akar," Jessica said.

"Yes. So rapid was their conquest that their leader believed himself a god, destined to rule all that he could conquer. Although I believe he claimed to be *uniting* the people he conquered."

"How did they manage such rapid conquest?" Jessica asked.

"None of the other worlds had thought to arm themselves," Tug explained. "None had thought it necessary."

Nathan couldn't help but think of the Earth, and how his father was running for office in order to stop the military buildup that he and so many others feared would provoke the Jung Dynasty into a preemptive invasion of Earth.

"When did the Doctrine of Origins begin?" Jessica asked.

"Not until after the Ta'Akar had also taken control of the systems surrounding the Pentaurus cluster. That's when Caius Ta'Akar declared himself lord and ruler of all worlds."

"That's a bit narcissistic," Jessica mumbled. "And no one tried to stop him?"

"Not at first. The Doctrine was so brutally enforced that no one dared defy it for fear of execution. Entire cities were leveled from space as a show of intolerance. It was a time of great madness and despair."

"But the rebellion, these people refuse to follow the doctrine?" Nathan asked.

"The rebellion is not so much about refusing to believe in the Doctrine of Origins, Captain. No one really cares where we came from. The rebellion is about not being forced to believe the ramblings of a self-appointed potentate. The Ta'Akar have managed to paint the rebels as a group of fundamentalist terrorists in the eyes of the public. But do not be fooled. The rebellion is about freedom—nothing more, nothing less. The Legends of Origin versus the Doctrine—that's really just a symbol of injustice and oppression."

Nathan paused a moment before speaking. Being a student of history, he found the tale fascinating. His current concern, however, was how it affected his people, his ship, and more importantly, his world. "That's an interesting tale, Mister Tugwell, but you still haven't answered my question. If we *were* from Earth, what would it mean to *you*?"

"To me personally? Nothing. It would be an interesting revelation, to say the least. I mean, to have something that has heretofore been considered only a legend *proven* to be true?" Tug contemplated the idea for a moment. "On second thought," Tug nodded, "I guess that might have a profound impact on me personally. As for what impact it might have on others? That's also a complicated question,

Captain."

Tug leaned forward, his elbows resting on the table, bringing himself closer to the others as if to emphasize his words. "But if you were from Earth, and the Ta'Akar knew this, then your lives would be in grave danger."

Nathan sensed the seriousness in Tug's voice. "Why? How are *we* a threat to *them*?"

His slip did not go unnoticed by Tug, whose eyes widened at the inadvertent confirmation, causing him to exclaim something in his own tongue. Nathan immediately realized, as did Jessica, that he had let the cat out of the bag.

"Then you *are* from Earth?" Tug exclaimed. "Captain, Caius will see you as a direct threat to his sovereignty. Do you not see? You are proof that his doctrine is nothing but lies. When word of your arrival spreads—and trust me, Captain, it will—the people will rise up once more. It will be the end of Caius and his regime!"

"Or a fucking slaughter!" Jessica interrupted.

"Jess!"

"No! Nathan, you heard him before. They glassed cities from space just to make a point. What do you think they'll do over this? What do you think they'll do to us?"

"They will not harm your ship," Jalea insisted.

"Bullshit! They'll frag us good and leave no traces."

"It is highly probable that they already know of your jump drive technology," Jalea explained, "in which case they will want to capture your ship in one piece."

"What is this jump drive?" Tug asked. Jalea began explaining to Tug in their native tongue, but before she got more than a few words out, Jessica jumped to her feet, her sidearm out and pointed at Jalea's head.

"You need to shut the fuck up, right now!" Jessica commanded.

"Whoa! Jess!" Nathan said, his hands coming up in surrender. She wasn't pointing her weapon at him, but it was right in front of his face at the moment. "What the hell are you doing?"

"She's telling him about the jump drive, Nathan!"

Suddenly, there was a high-pitched whining sound coming from the kitchen door. Jessica glanced to her left and saw Tug's wife, Ranni, standing in the doorway with an energy weapon pointed at Jessica's head, ready to fire.

Jessica turned her weapon a few inches to the left, training it on Tug instead of Jalea. "This weapon here, this one's not exactly standard issue," Jessica explained calmly, more for Ranni's benefit than anyone else's. "I adjusted the sensitivity on the trigger myself. It takes only the slightest pull to fire." Jessica turned her gaze directly to Tug's eyes, her own eyes narrowing into slits conveying the sense that she was ready for action. "When she shoots me, you'd better hope I don't flinch."

For several long seconds, everyone was silent, as each thought about their options. Finally, Nathan spoke. "All right," he started in a low and calm voice, "everyone needs to just relax and take a deep breath." Nathan looked at Jessica. "Tell me what's wrong, Jess."

"The little rebel princess here needs to stop blabbin' about things that aren't her business," Jessica explained.

"Okay, that makes sense, I guess."

"I apologize if I misspoke, Captain," Jalea said.

"Apology accepted," Nathan responded, holding up his hand to signal Jalea that it was not a good time for her to speak. "Now, how about we all just lower our weapons, and talk this out like civilized adults, okay?" Nathan looked at Jessica. "Is that okay with you, Jess?"

"I will if she will," Jessica said.

Nathan looked at Tug. "Will she, Tug?"

Tug looked to his wife, nodding for her to comply. She began to slowly lower her weapon, switching it off as it came down. Jessica heard the sound of Ranni's weapon charge winding down and began lowering her own weapon as well. Once her weapon was back in its holster under her cloak, Tug spoke up.

"I think I should tell you something, Captain. I am holding a weapon under the table, which I will now place *on* the table for all to see." Tug moved his hand slowly, revealing a small energy weapon that he held between his thumb and forefinger, dangling it in a position that was as non-threatening as possible. He placed the weapon on the table in front of him. "In the interest of good will," he said with a smile. "I apologize, Captain, but we live far from the city, and we do not know you or your people very well."

"No problem," Nathan promised. "I understand your precautions. Now, shall we all sit and resume our discussion?" Nathan began to sit down, Jessica following his lead.

"Stand down," Jessica announced over her comm-set. Nathan looked quizzically at Jessica, whose eyes glanced over at the window behind Tug. Outside the window, standing on the dark front porch, was

Vladimir. In his right hand he held his close-quarters weapon and had it pointed through the window at Tug and his wife. In his left hand was his handgun, which was raised and trained on someone Nathan could not see. He could only assume it was Danik. Vladimir winked at them as he lowered his weapons. The sight was a little unnerving to Nathan, as until now he had never seen his friend and cabin-mate as anything but a gregarious, fun-loving guy who was great at keeping their ship running. After shaking the sight off, Nathan looked back at Jessica.

"Oops," she said sheepishly. "Must've left my mic open."

"Captain," Tug began, "perhaps it would be best if we were just honest with each other. This dancing around, trying to gain a superior position, is getting tiresome. Do you not agree?"

"Yes, I do," Nathan admitted.

"Nathan," Jessica started, "if you're going..."

"Don't make me pull rank on you, Jess," he warned. Nathan looked at her sternly, before turning back to face Tug. "Yes, Tug, we are from Earth. But we're here by accident. We were testing an experimental faster-than-light propulsion system that we call a jump drive. With this, we can jump as far as ten light years in the blink of an eye."

Tug looked at him in disbelief. "But Captain, Earth is much farther than..."

"Yes, it is, a lot farther. But something happened. We were attacked by some Jung ships, and there was an anti-matter explosion just as we jumped away. To make a long story short, we ended up in the Pentaurus cluster. From what we've learned so far, it appears we jumped right into the middle of the rebellion's last stand."

Tug looked at Nathan, his mouth agape. He looked at Jalea next, hoping for some indication that it was all a joke. "It was you," Tug whispered to himself. "We heard that someone had intervened, allowing a few to escape capture. That was *you*?" He looked at Jalea again, who nodded. "Oh, Captain, you are definitely in danger. The rumors are that a mysterious ship simply appeared in the middle of the battle, destroyed a Ta'Akar capital ship, and then simply vanished. There is surely a bounty on your ship by now. Every half-witted criminal with delusions of grandeur will be looking for you. And you're sitting right in the middle of the biggest collection of ne'er-do-wells the galaxy has ever seen."

"Great," Jessica said. "We're in it up to our eyeballs, yet again."

"Well at least we know about it now," Nathan added.

"Captain," Tug added, leaning forward once again, "did any of the Ta'Akar ships *see* you jump away?"

"Yeah," Nathan said, looking at Jessica, unsure of the number, "at least one, maybe two. I'm not sure."

"Jalea is correct. If they have realized you have the ability to jump between the stars, they will stop at nothing to obtain this technology." Tug could see by the look in Nathan's eyes that he did not see the seriousness of the situation. "You said you were hit by an anti-matter explosion just as you jumped?"

"Yes."

"And that it propelled you much farther than you thought possible?"

"That's the working theory, so I'm told."

"When the Ta'Akar figure this all out, they will

want to combine your jump drive with their new power source. With that combination, they will become an unstoppable power." Tug shook his head in disbelief. "You must destroy it, Captain."

"Destroy what?"

"The jump drive!"

"Are you nuts?" Nathan cried, suddenly standing. "That's our only way of getting home."

"It's the only way to be sure…"

"You don't understand," Nathan interrupted. "It's one of a kind. There are no others back on Earth. There's not even a record of it. That drive is the only hope my world has of repelling an invasion."

Tug looked Nathan squarely in the eyes. "If the Ta'Akar capture your jump drive, Captain, these Jung you speak of will be the least of your problems."


The front door of Tug's home swung open wildly as Nathan burst out onto the front porch, stumbling down the steps. Jessica came running out of the house right behind him, with Jalea and Tug close on her heels.

"Nathan! Where are you going?" Jessica yelled.

"We've gotta get back to the ship!" Nathan muttered as he walked out into the amber twilight. "We've gotta get outta here, now!" He suddenly realized he was headed nowhere and stopped dead in his tracks. His mind was spinning. He had to clear his head. He needed to be able to think more clearly. His people, his ship, and his world were all in danger, and he had to do… something.

Nathan spun around to face the others. "Jalea, call Tobin and tell him to pick us up."

"Of course," she responded.

"Jess, round everyone up. It's time to go."

Jessica looked around. They were all standing right there, even Vladimir and Danik who had heard the commotion and come back from the far end of the compound.

"Good, you're all here," Nathan said, as he saw Vladimir and Danik approach.

"Tobin is not answering," Jalea informed him.

"It's just as well, Captain," Tug assured him. "A ship coming out here at this late hour would surely raise suspicion."

"Okay," Nathan said, thinking of another plan. "A ride, then. Can you give us a ride back to town?"

"To what end?"

"We can meet Tobin there, at the spaceport." Nathan was beginning to sound desperate.

"And if he is not there?" Jalea asked.

"We can wait for him," Nathan said.

"It would be safer for you to wait here, Captain," Tug assured him, "away from the very types that would hand you over to the Ta'Akar for the reward."

"Jalea?" Nathan pleaded. "Anything?"

"He is not answering, I'm afraid."

"Jess, raise the ship," Nathan ordered, becoming slightly more rational. "Tell them what's going on, and see if they can raise Tobin on the comms."

"Yes, sir," Jessica answered. She began to step away slowly, passing in front of Vladimir. "Keep an eye on him," she whispered.

"Do not worry," Vladimir promised. He moved closer to his friend. "Nathan, what is wrong?"

"We're fucked, Vlad," Nathan admitted under his breath.

"What do you mean? Why?"

"If what Tug says is true, then every Tom, Dick,

and Ta'Akar in this sector is going to be hunting for us. And we're too busted up to fight them all off, Vlad."

"Then we will simply jump away again," he told him, "and we will keep jumping all the way back to Sol if we have to, ten light years at a time." Vladimir put his right hand on Nathan's shoulder. "And they will never catch up to us," he promised, patting Nathan's cheek with his other hand. "You worry too much, Nathan. We will be fine; you will see."

Nathan looked his friend in the eyes. Nathan envied Vladimir his strength, his confidence. No matter what fate threw at him, Vladimir took it head on without hesitation. "I don't know what to do," Nathan admitted quietly to his friend.

"You will figure it out, Nathan."

"What if I'm wrong?"

"Then you will figure out another way," Vladimir told him. "Now straighten up, hold your chin high, and stop whining," he joked. "Is embarrassing."

Nathan looked at Vladimir as a smile formed across the Russian's face. He made a face at Nathan, like he was pouting, mocking him. "Right," Nathan laughed. Nathan tapped his comm-set to open the microphone. "Jess, tell the ship we're spending the night here. Have them locate Tobin and tell him to be ready to run cargo and passengers from this location to the ship tomorrow around..." Nathan looked at Tug for an approximate time.

"Around midday?" Tug suggested.

"Midday," Nathan continued. "And tell them we'll check back with them later before we turn in." Nathan keyed off his microphone, turning to Tug. "Mister Tugwell, we'll be taking you up on your kind offer to stay the night, but we will be departing tomorrow."

"You are still buying my molo, aren't you?"

Nathan smiled. "Of course."

"I do have one request, Captain," Tug added.

"And what might that be?"

"Would you tell me more about your world?"

"Of course," Nathan said, as he started back for the house.

# CHAPTER SIX

Nathan stepped out onto the front porch of Tug's house. He had spent the last two hours telling Tug all about the Earth—from how they had first colonized the core systems, to the bio-digital plague that nearly destroyed all of humanity. He had told him about the centuries of despair that had followed the great plague, and about how the Earth had gone through a rapid development spurt since the Data Ark had been discovered a century ago.

Tug had hung on his every word, like a child being told a magical story of a faraway land. The entire time, Nathan couldn't help but feel like he was solving a mystery in Tug's mind, like it was the piece to a puzzle that he had been missing all his life, preventing him from finding true satisfaction. It had been an unexpected experience for the both of them. By the time they had finished, Tug surely knew more about Earth than any native in the entire quadrant.

Nathan wondered if he had told Tug too much. Had Jessica been there, he was sure she would've thought so. But Tug had wanted the information and more. Nathan couldn't quite figure out why the knowledge of Earth had been so important to the farmer. He wondered how many more people Tug would eventually share his knowledge of Earth with. These people had no understanding of their true origins. They had myths. They had stories. They had legends. But no truths. In some small measure, Nathan felt he had done this world a bit of justice.

Nathan stretched and took in a deep breath. The air was different out here in the country night. It was still thick and humid, and it still smelled of molo. But the smells of machine oils and thrust exhausts and all the other aromas one usually found amongst civilization were absent, as were the sounds. It was quiet out here, almost too quiet. On Earth, there were always sounds. Even in the wilderness, there were always the sounds of hundreds of creatures big and small, as they went about the business of life. On this reformed moon, however, those creatures were almost nonexistent, as were their sounds. The silence was... peaceful.

He looked about the compound spotting Jessica a short distance away, squatting on the ground as she assembled the tight beam comm-array dish used to communicate privately with the Aurora.

"Jess," he called, walking out to meet her, "contact the ship yet?"

"Just getting ready to."

Nathan walked the last few steps over to her. "You get a good look around?"

"What makes you think I was looking around?"

"Why do you think I made you my security chief?"

"Because I was one of the few people on board that you actually knew by name."

"What did you find out?"

Jessica stood up, having finished assembling the array. "There's something not right about this place," she said.

"What do you mean, not right? It looks pretty normal to me."

"Yeah, it does, but I found a few things that don't add up."

"Such as?"

"Such as why is there only one vehicle? You'd think with this many greenhouses there would be more than one vehicle to haul his harvest to market."

"He can only drive one vehicle at a time, Jess."

"He must have help from time to time. Otherwise, why would he have a bunkhouse out back? Even if he was the only driver, you'd think there would at least be a trailer."

Nathan thought about it for a moment. Jessica had a naturally suspicious mind, which is why she was perfect for the job. "Maybe it gets picked up."

"Maybe, but there's more. Considering the amount of harvest he should be producing, you'd think he'd be a little wealthier. Either he's stashing his money away, or he's giving his crops away on the cheap."

"That just makes him either a smart businessman, or a really bad one."

"Okay, then how about all the emitters?"

"Emitters?" That got Nathan's attention.

"They're implanted into the sides of the sinkhole walls all the way around the compound, nearly up to ground level."

"What kind of emitters?"

"Couldn't tell. But they've got to be either shield emitters or some kind of sensor scattering field."

"Maybe they're just to repel insects." Nathan chuckled.

"Yeah, right. Laugh it up. But, you know that damaged fighter of his? The one he supposedly scavenged over the years? Well it's not as damaged as he led us to believe. It looks old and beaten up all right—and it's obviously been in one hell of a fire fight—but Vlad thinks the battle damage is recent. And get this; he also thinks it's still space-worthy."

"I thought he said he sold the reactor to buy this farm."

"Maybe he did. Maybe he replaced it later. Maybe that's what he spent all his money on. But the ship's got two, now, and they're both still good. Vlad thinks you could light them up and take off in minutes." Jessica waited for Nathan to poke holes in her final report.

"Okay, that is odd."

"And one other thing, Nathan. The markings on the ship. I'm pretty sure they're the same ones I saw on the uniforms of that boarding party we fought off down on C deck."

"Are you sure?"

"Five-point star inside a circle. Kind of hard to mistake. I think that's a Ta'Akar fighter in there."

"He did say that there were mass defections amongst the troops. Maybe he was one of them."

"Or maybe he's a spy," Jessica suggested.

"Okay, that's a scary thought," Nathan admitted.

"To be honest," Jessica admitted, "it doesn't add up."

"What do you mean?"

"I mean using this farming gig as a cover. For a spy, it's a lousy choice. You spend far more time on the farm than in town. And when you are in town, you're stuck in a street market. Not gonna gather much intel that way. But then again, maybe he's not supposed to. Maybe he's just here in case they need an operative."

"You're not making me feel any better, Jess."

"I recommend we keep a watch during the night,

just to be safe."

"Agreed. Update the Aurora. I'm going to go and have a look at that ship for myself."

* * *

"We made contact with Tobin," Cameron told Jessica over the comm link. "Claims he was subjected to a surprise inspection of his ship by the port authority and had to shut down his comms for awhile."

*"You believe him?"*

"Sounds logical enough, but he was off the air for several hours. Seems like a rather lengthy inspection. He agreed it was safer for you to spend the night there rather than raise suspicion with a late night pickup, especially after the surprise inspection."

*"Okay then. We'll check back in four hours. Nash out."*

Cameron motioned for the comm officer to close the channel. The landing party had been gone for eight hours, which was considerably longer than any of them had expected. And now they were going to be gone at least another fourteen hours. It had been relatively uneventful, with the harvesting operations running smoothly. The workers had already ferried three full loads of ore to the surface to be sold at market, which Tobin assured her was enough to pay the harvesters their fees and expenses. And since the workers intended to continue through the night, they would have more than enough to pay for the food Nathan was purchasing the next day.

"Kaylah, it's going to be a long night, and you've got a lot of traffic to monitor, so why don't you take a break. Maybe take a catnap or something. I'll cover your station until you get back."

"What about you, sir?" Kaylah asked. "You've been on duty just as long."

"I'm good," Cameron assured her. "I don't sleep much anyway. Besides, I'll crash out in the ready room when you return. Now go, before I change my mind."

"Yes, sir," Kaylah said as she rose to take leave.

Cameron sat down in Kayla's place, taking a good long look at the sensor display. It was a sea of contacts—a mixture of rock and ice, interspersed with ships of various sizes. The smaller ones, probably harvesters, were darting about, while the larger sat in or near the rings as they waited for their harvesters to feed their holds. It was a mass of confusion and very difficult to track with so much activity. She shook her head, making a mental note to herself; if Kaylah was going to double as their sensor officer for a time, she was going to need some additional training in how to better configure her displays. She immediately began color coding the contacts, assigning green to non-threats and orange to contacts to be watched. There were only two contacts that warranted a red color, both of which were local patrol ships owned by the family. They had both been patrolling just outside the rings the entire time. Cameron could not determine their intent, but as they were the only vessels with any significant offensive weaponry, they would have to be watched at all times. Cameron knew that if either of those two patrol ships got close enough to get a good look at them, they would quickly realize that they were not a Volonese cargo ship. That was a possibility that she didn't like to think about.

* * *

Ensign Mendez sat on a packing crate along the side of the hangar bay, observing the harvesting operations. His eyelids were drooping, his fatigue evident as he struggled to stay alert. Marcus, the harvesting crew foreman, approached. Mendez straightened up, forcing his eyes to open wider and appear more alert. He didn't much care for the old man, especially after watching him berate his workers the entire time they had been on board.

Marcus was wide awake and was happily gnawing away on something that resembled a small, ugly carrot. "Past your bedtime, boy?"

"Just wish I had some coffee," Ensign Mendez muttered.

"What's coffee?"

"A hot beverage that helps keep you awake."

"Well go get yourself some. We ain't goin' nowhere."

"Can't. We ran out."

"Too bad. You say it keeps you awake?"

"Yeah."

"Here," Marcus pulled another of the strange looking tubers from his pocket and tossed it to Mendez, "munch on that awhile."

Mendez barely managed to catch the tuber as it struck his chest. "What is it?"

"Just think of it as coffee on a stick," Marcus laughed. "You can thank me later," he added as he returned to his work.

Mendez held the scraggly looking tuber up in front of his face. On closer inspection, it didn't appear to be a tuber at all. It was actually a small twig covered with a densely compacted collection of gelatinous drops, mostly colored pale oranges and yellows. He sniffed it but found no noticeable aroma. He tried pinching one of the drops but found it was firmer than it looked. He pulled one of them off, and after inspection, decided to give it a try. It was crunchy, a texture reminiscent of a peanut. It had a rather bitter taste to it which, although tolerable, was not pleasant. Having survived the first taste, he repeated the process until he had devoured nearly half the stick.

A few moments later, Mendez found himself up and walking around, unable to sit still with his newfound energy coursing through his veins. He looked at Marcus as he passed by, nodding his thanks. Marcus smiled and laughed. "Don't eat too much! You'll be climbing the walls!"

* * *

"This little ship is amazing," Vladimir said. Nathan hadn't seen his friend so excited since he first learned of the jump drive the special projects team had installed on board the Aurora. He stood at the doorway of the barn in which the ship was housed. It was smaller than he had thought, only about twenty meters long and maybe ten meters wide at the most. It resembled an old flying wing design and looked like a stretched out, flattened triangle, with two massive engine pods sitting on its wings on either side of the cigar-shaped fuselage that only protruded slightly ahead of the main wing shape. The cockpit canopy was only a slight protrusion sticking up from the fuselage with view ports cut into its front and sides.

Nathan followed Vladimir up the boarding ladder to the cockpit. From ground level, Nathan had only seen the top of one flight seat, but once he made it to the top of the ladder, he could see that there was a second seat tucked in behind the first.

"There is so much packed into this little ship," Vladimir explained. "Energy and projectile weapons, reflective shielding, anti-gravity lift systems, inertial dampeners..." Vladimir had to stop to catch his breath. "Nathan, it even has limited FTL capabilities."

"This ship has FTL?"

"Yes. But even without the FTL, it can still outrun the Aurora's sub-light drive."

"What kind of propulsion system does it use?"

"The reactors are fusion. That much I know. But the main propulsion systems, I have no idea."

"Doesn't Danik know?"

"I'm not sure. Maybe he does, maybe not. I do not fully understand everything he says as yet," Vladimir admitted.

Nathan wondered if Danik was as difficult to get information out of as Jalea had been. It would make sense, with both of them being from the same organization. It might be doctrine not to reveal too much information. It certainly was Jessica's preferred method of operation. And it was a skill Nathan had yet to master.

Nathan stepped back down the ladder, backing away from the ship as he stepped back onto the dirt. The ship had several impact marks where it had obviously been struck with weapons fire. There was also charring around the nearest engine pod, probably from an internal fire. "And you think this thing is still space-worthy?"

"Yes, I am almost certain of this."

"You think the technology on this little ship would be of value to us?"

"The compact nature of her FTL systems alone would be of great value. Maybe not to us, but definitely to the fleet."

"I wonder if Tug would be willing to sell it to us."

"Oh, Nathan," Vladimir drooled, "do not tease me."

\* \* \*

Nathan entered the small bunkhouse behind the main house. It was a simple building of wood, clay, and rock construction similar to the others. The floor, although it looked like dirt, was fused solid and smooth in a way that Nathan had never seen. There were ten modest beds of wood-frame construction, a pair on each side of the main entrance with six more along the back wall. Each bed was covered with a heavy woven cloth blanket.

Nathan entered the bunkhouse, turning to his right to head toward what he hoped was a door to the bathroom at the far end. The room was lit with softly glowing pale-white lighting panels above the head of each bed, casting a soft and relaxing glow in semi-circles around them. There were larger, overhead lighting panels spread across the beamed ceiling of the room, however, these were not lit.

The room appeared relaxing and comfortable, despite its overall rustic nature, and Nathan looked forward to getting some rest after a long and somewhat emotionally exhausting day. He came to the end of the room and reached out to take hold of the doorknob to what he assumed was the bathroom door, when it suddenly swung open away from him, startling him.

"Oh, Nathan," Jalea said, a bit surprised herself. "I didn't realize anyone else was here yet."

Nathan stepped back out of surprise. Jalea had removed much of her outer clothing and was dressed only in a tight-fitting body suit that was rolled down to a few centimeters below her navel and an old, worn undershirt that covered most of her upper torso. Nathan had always been captivated by Jalea's eyes. In fact, their effect on him had caused him to question his own decisions to place trust in her from time to time. As she had always been dressed in loosely fitted clothing, he had not noticed her voluptuous figure until now.

"Excuse me. I didn't mean to intrude," Nathan apologized. For some reason, he was embarrassed, despite the fact that she was still fully dressed. Nathan turned and stepped over to the nearest bed, taking off his cloak and dropping it on the bed.

Jalea moved past him, turning down the bed next to his. Nathan watched her out of the corner of his eye. The skin on her lower back was the same olive complexion as her face. She was not like most of the women he had known. For the last four years, Nathan had only dated classmates from the fleet academy. Most of them had been the athletic type, all toned and muscled from the hours of intense physical training that they were subjected to during their time on campus. This woman was softer, more curvaceous than he could ever remember seeing.

"Tug seems like a good man," Nathan said, trying to distract himself from Jalea's ample charms.

Jalea climbed into her bed, "Yes, he is that." She pulled her blanket just up to her hips, making no effort to cover herself as she lay on her side facing him. "I believe he found your tales of Earth quite interesting," she told him as she propped her head up on one hand, her elbow against the bed, "as did I." She looked at him a long moment as he removed his jumpsuit, stripping down to just his standard-issue uniform pants and fleet undershirt. "You seem to know a great deal of Earth history. Are all your people so knowledgeable?"

"It was my major," he explained, realizing that she probably wouldn't know what he meant. "It was my area of focus during my formal education."

"A rather fortunate coincidence, as you have become an emissary for your world."

"Yes, I suppose it is."

"Did your engineer find Tug's ship interesting?"

"Very much so," Nathan told her. "Actually, I was thinking of asking Tug if he would be willing to part with it."

"I doubt that would be the case," she assured him.

"You wouldn't think a farmer would have much use for a space fighter."

"Perhaps," she admitted, "but Tug is not your average molo farmer."

"How so?" Nathan asked, sitting on the side of his bed facing her.

"Do not misunderstand me; there are many like him—men who have spent years fighting for the cause of others who then give it all up to lead a more simple life. I can cite many examples, albeit not on Haven, mind you. However, I would think that if the ship was of no use to him, he would have parted with it long ago."

Nathan nodded agreement, having not thought that far yet. "You may be right."

At that moment, the main door swung open and

Jessica walked in. Jalea immediately pulled her blanket up to cover herself, laying her head down on her rolled up cloak. "I suppose it would not hurt to ask, however."

Jessica eyed them both suspiciously as she approached. "I made contact with the ship," she told him.

Nathan rose and headed for the bathroom, with Jessica following him. "You got them up to speed?"

"Yes, sir. Cameron said Tobin had some problem with the port authority, which put him out of contact for several hours."

"Sound right to you?" Nathan asked as they entered the bathroom.

"Could be," she said, following him into the bathroom. She fumbled around the faucet for a moment. "How the hell do you turn the water on?" Finally, after tapping the top of the faucet, the water began to run. "Something just isn't right, Nathan," she whispered, hoping the sound of the running water would mask their conversation.

"What do you mean?" Nathan whispered back.

"Why this world? Why Tobin? Why Tug? Oh, and Tug just happens to have a Ta'Akar fighter, and a compound equipped with emitters. And let us not forget the gun strapped to the underside of his dinner table." Jessica looked at Nathan, waiting for him to put it together.

"What? You think this is all planned? By who?" Nathan stared at her, waiting for a response that never came. Instead, Jessica glanced back toward the door. "Jalea?" Nathan laughed.

"Who else?" Jessica asked.

"When did she have time to put this all together, Jess?"

"She had plenty of time alone with Tobin back on

the Aurora. And they seemed a bit too buddy-buddy for just business acquaintances."

"Oh, come on. Don't you think you're reaching a bit?"

"*Oh, Nathan,*" Jessica whispered in a mock-sexy voice. "*Do not misunderstand me; Tug is a simple farmer. Good and honorable...*"

"What were you doing, listening from outside the door?" Nathan's eyes widened.

"Of course not," she insisted. "I bugged the room more than an hour ago."

"Jesus, Jess. Is this how all spec-ops operate?"

"The good ones, yeah. Just don't let her fool you with her sexy green eyes and her big tits."

"What?"

"Oh, you know what I'm talking about, Nathan."

"What am I, sixteen?"

"No, but you are a guy. And all guys tend to think with their dicks."

"I'm not that simpleminded," Nathan defended.

"Bullshit. It took me all of three minutes to get your pants off, remember?" she told him as she rinsed her hands in the running water.

"I was drunk," he reminded her.

"Maybe. But your dick wasn't, and that's my point. Just be wary; that's all I'm saying. Jalea does everything for a reason, Nathan. And you need to keep that in mind at all times." Jessica dried her hands off on her cloak as she spoke. "Now clear out. I've gotta use the can," she ordered, pushing him toward the door.

"Just close the stall door," he suggested, not quite ready to leave.

"That molo did not agree with me," she warned. "Trust me. You want to clear the room," she added, pushing him toward the door.

# CHAPTER SEVEN

Nathan and Vladimir sat on the bench on the porch of the bunkhouse. Nathan's watch had ended just as the sun was coming up, and Vladimir and Danik had only just returned from spending their entire night examining the systems on Tug's fighter.

"She is correct, you know. All men are more easily manipulated by beautiful women, at least to some degree. Even if we do not want to admit to this, is true. But is not only this way for men. Women do this as well. Maybe not as much as us, but still."

"Then you think I only trust Jalea because she's attractive?"

"I think *because* you find her attractive, you are willing to assume she is trustworthy. If she had been old hag, you would've dismissed her without a thought. But that is to be expected, because you and I are men. That is how we are. If you know this about yourself, and you always question your motives, then you will be okay."

"Then Jessica was just reminding me to check my motives?"

"Yes, I believe so."

"Not exactly the way you treat your captain though, is it?"

"Nathan, you have been captain for less than one week. To us, you are *still* ensign. You must *earn* their respect. It does not come with the bars, you know."

Nathan thought about it as Tug approached, carrying a steaming hot pot and a stack of bowls.

"Good day, Nathan," Tug called. "I brought your morning meal," he added, setting the pot and bowls down on the bench next to them. "It is not much, just a simple porridge I'm afraid. But it is very filling and should get you through the day."

"I'm sure it will be fine," Nathan assured him. "Thank you."

Vladimir was already scooping up a bowl full and shoveling it into his mouth. "Kasha. It tastes like Kasha."

"Tug," Nathan continued, "we were wondering if you'd be interested in selling your ship."

"Oh, no. I don't think I could part with it. Besides, what use do you have for such a small vessel? Your ship is a hundred times its size."

"There are some interesting systems on your ship that we'd love to study. We might be able to integrate some of your technology into our own systems, possibly give us additional advantages."

"I'm sorry, Captain. Perhaps I can let you have one or two of her redundant systems. Say, a shield emitter, or one of the pulse cannons. Perhaps they would be helpful."

Vladimir nodded. "Better than nothing, I suppose. I was hoping to get a better look at your FTL system."

"Well, you still have several hours until your friend arrives," Tug said. "Perhaps you can spend it examining the FTL drive."

"I'm afraid it would take me much longer than a few hours to understand it," Vladimir admitted.

"I will send my oldest daughter, Deliza, to help you," Tug boasted. "She is quite knowledgeable in such matters."

"Any help would be appreciated," Vladimir assured him between spoonfuls of porridge.

"Very well. I shall send her to you after her morning chores are completed," Tug promised. "Now, Captain, if you'll excuse me. I have my own chores to complete. I will return later and we can begin preparing your purchase for shipment."

"Thank you," He watched Tug walk back toward the main house. "Looks like you've got yourself an FTL tutor."

Vladimir said nothing. He just kept eating.

\* \* \*

Tobin's ship kicked up dust in all directions as it hovered a few meters off the ground, slowly rotating to point its nose back in the direction it had come before it settled to the ground in the middle of Tug's compound. Nathan, Jessica, Jalea, and Tug all huddled behind Tug's vehicle to shield themselves from the whirling dust and debris as Tobin's ship settled to the ground and its engines began to spin down. Nathan looked around, noticing that the dust was slow to disperse.

"This is why I don't usually fly purchases out!" Tug yelled over the declining sound of Tobin's engines. "It takes forever for the dust to clear! One of the disadvantages of living in a big hole!" Tug pulled his shirt up to cover his mouth and nose to avoid breathing in the dust as he rose from behind the vehicle. Nathan did the same as he followed.

The large cargo hatch on the starboard side of Tobin's ship swung down until it touched the dirt, becoming a loading ramp on which Tobin quickly descended. "Captain! It's good to see you safe."

"Why wouldn't we be?" he asked.

"This is Haven, Captain. *Safe* describes very little on this world," he smiled. "Shall we begin loading?"

"Tobin, this is Tug," Nathan introduced. "I believe we should first settle our bill with him."

"Yes, of course," Tobin agreed, feigning forgetfulness. Tobin produced a small bag from under his cloak. "This should more than cover it," he told them as he handed the bag to Tug.

Tug took the bag from Tobin. Surprised by the excessive weight, he opened the bag to look inside and found many more credit chips than he had expected. "This is too generous, Captain."

"Consider it a bonus for all your hospitality," Nathan told him.

"But Captain, this is nearly twice what the molo is worth at market."

"Yeah, well, we did almost blow your head off last night," Nathan chuckled. "So I think you deserve it. Maybe it will get your wife off your back for letting a bunch of strangers stay for dinner."

"Indeed it might," he agreed as he tucked the bag of credit chips into his pants pocket.

"We should get going as soon as possible," Tobin insisted, seeming a bit anxious.

"Of course." Nathan turned to the others and signaled them to start loading the bundles of molo.

They quickly hauled the carefully tied bundles up into Tobin's ship, stacking them down the middle of the small passenger area.

"Stack them wall to wall, Captain," Tobin advised.

"How are we all going to fit on board if we do that?"

"I would prefer to take the cargo up separately,"

Tobin explained. "It would be safer as there is no good way to secure the load. If we were to hit some turbulence, someone could become injured by flying bundles."

Nathan looked about the cabin, comparing the available space with the amount of cargo still to load. Although he figured there would be enough room to squeeze them all in along with the cargo, he figured it was better to follow Tobin's advice and err on the side of caution. And since Vladimir had not completed his study of the FTL systems on Tug's fighter, the additional time would not be wasted. "Okay, wall to wall it is."

Ten minutes later, the ship was loaded and ready to go. "Very well, Captain," Tobin announced. "I will run this load up to your ship and return for you in just over an hour." Tobin waved as he climbed back up into his ship, the loading ramp swinging up behind him and filling in the hatch as it sealed shut.

Nathan and the others again moved behind the vehicle as Tobin's ship began to spin up its engines. Within minutes, the whine of the turbines was replaced by the roar of the thrusters as it lifted off, ascending vertically until it was well above the top of the sinkhole before it began to turn and accelerate forward. They could no longer see it through the cloud of dust that enveloped them, but the sound of his engines quickly disappeared.

"My wife will be complaining about the dust for days," Tug groaned as he brushed himself off.

"Jess, contact the ship and tell them that Tobin is on his way with the first load. And let her know we'll be back on board in a couple hours. I'm going to go check on Vlad."

\* \* \*

"Commander," Ensign Yosef said, "one of the cargo shuttles just departed on another run to Haven."

"Again? That's their fourth load today," Cameron said. "How much stuff is he buying down there?" Cameron twisted from side to side in the command chair. It had been a long night, and her attempts to take naps on the ready room couch had left her a bit stiff. "Any sign of Tobin yet?"

"He left Haven spaceport about an hour ago. He set down on the surface about thirty kilometers outside of the city for about fifteen minutes. I'm assuming that's the landing party's current location, as Ensign Nash contacted us just after Tobin lifted off again to inform us he was inbound with cargo— something called molo. He should be arriving in a few minutes. I show him entering the rings now..."

Kaylah's voice suddenly stopped in mid sentence, drawing Cameron's attention. "What is it?"

"That's odd," Kaylah said. She double checked her readings before continuing. "I could've sworn I saw a rather large contact. But it's gone now."

"Did you get an ID on it?"

"No, sir. It was only on my screen for an instant before it disappeared. The system didn't even have time to generate a track log for it."

"A ghost? A false contact of some sort, maybe?" Cameron theorized.

"Possibly, but I'm pretty sure it was a legitimate contact." Kaylah turned to face Cameron. "It might have slipped behind the planet, dropping out of our line of sight before we could get a fix on it."

"Is that possible?"

"I've seen a few contacts come out from behind the planet that I didn't see going in. I just assumed they had arrived on the far side."

"How long until it would come out from behind and be visible again?"

"About an hour at normal orbital velocities," Kaylah reported.

"Well, it's not like we can go and investigate," Cameron said. "Keep an eye peeled in case it comes back."

"Yes, sir."

* * *

"How much longer are you going to hide?" Jalea pleaded. She and Tug stood in the middle of the bunkhouse, arguing.

"For the rest of my life!" Tug insisted. "The rebellion is over, Jalea. You just refuse to accept defeat."

"You once said that as long as you could still hold a weapon, you would continue to fight! What has changed?"

"We no longer *hold* a weapon!" he told her. "We have no ships, and maybe twenty surviving members who have scattered to the winds! And if they are successful with their new power source, there will be no stopping them!"

"We have a weapon!" Jalea insisted. "Their ship! With their jump drive, we can appear within range of key targets, destroy them, and then disappear before they even have a chance to defend themselves!

"And how do you propose to attack with a broken ship? You said yourself it was badly damaged in its recent engagements. It has no energy weapons, no shields. It isn't even completed."

"We can fix their ship," she pleaded. "We can use our technology, give them energy weapons, improve their shields..."

"And how will you do this? With what army?" he asked.

"We can find our people. And when news of our magical victories begins to spread, more will join us and our ranks will swell once again."

"And why, Jalea? Tell me, why would *they* want to help our cause?" Tug asked, pointing outside.

"They *need* that power source. Without it, it will take them months to get home instead of weeks. And their world is also in dire need of their jump drive. Helping us will help them."

Tug stared at Jalea a moment. "You may be right. But still I cannot join you. I made a promise to Ranni and my children."

"You made a promise to your people, as well."

"Do not go there, Jalea. I fought as much as any man—more so! I was fighting when you were still in braided tails and studying Angla with your father. I have shed as much blood as any man could and still live to tell. This last battle was nearly my undoing. My wounds are still not yet fully healed. If I was to leave yet again, I do not think I would have a home to return to should I survive." Tug dropped to sit on the edge of one of the beds. "My days as a Karuzari are over, Jalea. It is time for another to pick up the flag in my place."

Jalea moved to sit on the bed next to him. She picked up his hand and held it in her own. "I do not mean to cast disrespect on all that you have done for our people; you know that. No man has fought more bravely than you. You have been an inspiration to many for more than two decades. And you will not be soon forgotten."

\* \* \*

Tobin nervously paced the hangar deck while Ensign Mendez and a few members of the Aurora's crew finished unloading the molo from his ship. The ensign noticed Tobin's anxiety and stopped to inquire. "Everything all right, Tobin?"

"Yes, yes, everything is fine. Why do you ask?"

"You seem a little anxious," Mendez told him.

"I'm just in a hurry to retrieve your crew from the surface," Tobin insisted.

"Yeah, you and the XO, both." Tobin ignored the ensign's words, returning to his ship, pretending to inspect one of his thrusters. As Mendez returned to the ship to carry another load, he watched Tobin. A few minutes later, Tobin's ship was unloaded. "That's the last of it," Mendez told Tobin.

"Excellent," Tobin declared, as he strode back up the ramp to his ship.

"Do you need any fuel or anything?" Mendez asked.

"No thank you, ensign. I have quite enough," he assured him as he headed for the cockpit.

Mendez headed down the ramp. No sooner had he stepped off the ramp than it began to fold back up into Tobin's ship. A moment later, his ship began to back up slowly, pivoting to bring its nose facing aft before it began to roll forward toward the transfer airlocks. Ensign Mendez was forced to quicken his stride in order to get clear of Tobin's ship. "Damn, that guy's in a hurry," Mendez exclaimed to the sergeant as he reached the edge of the bay.

\* \* \*

Just offshore, a small, unmarked ship sped toward the coastline. Even though its body never touched the water, its turbulent wake of thrust still parted the waters below as it hurtled across the shoreline and continued inward. Within seconds it reached Haven City, decelerating quickly as it approached the space port. No one challenged its arrival, and no one questioned its purpose. All who noticed it also knew they were better served to look away.

The ship bypassed the usual approach paths, instead skimming over the rows of berths until it reached its destination. Upon reaching its target, it dropped quickly to the deck, its landing gear extruding to full deployment a fraction of a second before the ship touched down, her boarding ramp deploying before she had even landed.

The cargo shuttle from the Aurora's harvesting crew had just finished offloading the shipment when the strange ship swooped down and landed next to them in their berth. It had been quite unexpected, and the pilot of the cargo shuttle was more than irritated.

"Who the hell do you think you are?" he hollered as he strode arrogantly toward the unmarked ship's boarding ramp. "This is a private..."

A blast from a well-aimed energy weapon ended both his sentence and his life as it struck him square in the chest, hurtling him backwards at least two meters. He landed in a smoking heap directly in front of the indentured workers he had been ordering about only a few seconds earlier. The workers stared in disbelief at the sizzling chest wound on the body of their pilot.

Their disbelief quickly turned to horror as a dozen assault troops clad in black and gray armor poured out of the unmarked ship, their silenced energy weapons firing in almost inaudible *clicks* as they quickly dispatched their targets with pinpoint accuracy. The attackers quickly fanned out to either side, their weapons quietly clicking as they fired. There were grunts and muffled cries from their victims, each one's life ending with the sound of their own sizzling wounds. Within seconds, the assault was over and the workers lay smoking on the tarmac in much the same condition as their pilot.

"Clear!" the lead soldier called out.

A moment later, their commanding officer stepped out of the ship, surveying the scene from the top of the boarding ramp. "Get rid of the bodies and clean this place up," he ordered as he descended the ramp. Another dozen troops deployed from the ship behind him. He turned around to see that the rest of his men had disembarked, then signaled to the pilot that he was clear to depart. The ships engines, which had not been shutdown, spun back up quickly and the ship lifted off once more, heading off deeper into the countryside.

*"Halo flight taking up control station inland,"* the pilot announced over the commander's comm-set.

"Copy that, Halo flight. Team two will contact you when they are ready for extraction." The commander strode into the middle of the berth, watching as his men dragged the bodies of the workers into the nearby buildings. "We've got ten minutes until the next ship arrives, so let's get to it!"

A few minutes later, the squad leader approached his commander. "All bodies are secure, sir," he reported as he snapped a salute.

"And your assault team?"

"Positioned undercover in the service building, sir."

"Very well," the commander said, turning to head toward the captured cargo shuttle. "Mount up!" he ordered. The two rows of eight fully armored troops ran up the rear loading ramp of the bulky old cargo shuttle that had belonged to the harvesting team.

The commander touched the comm-band around his neck and began to speak. "Halo flight, team one."

"*Go for Halo flight.*"

"Halo flight, team one. You may start the music."

"*Copy team one, starting the music.*"

The commander took one last glance around the berth as he turned and headed up the loading ramp into the cargo shuttle. Moments later, the old shuttle's engines spun up and it began to taxi out of the berth.


"Sir," Ensign Yosef called, "Tobin's shuttle is not headed for the same coordinates as before."

Cameron was standing behind the helm station and turned toward Kaylah. "Where's he headed then?"

"I'm not sure..."

"*XO, hangar bay,*" Cameron's comm-set interrupted.

"Go ahead, hangar bay," Cameron answered over her comm.

"*Mendez, sir. I'm not sure it means anything, but*

*Tobin was acting a little odd."*

"What do you mean, odd?"

"Sir," Ensign Yosef interrupted, "I think Tobin's headed for the spaceport."

*"He seemed anxious, like he was in a hurry,"* Mendez reported.

"Standby one," Cameron said over the comms before turning back to Kaylah. "Are you sure?"

"Well, the entry trajectory does suggest the port as his destination. But there isn't much difference between heading for Haven or heading to the countryside outside of Haven."

"There is if you're a pilot, Kaylah," Cameron insisted. "Maybe he's going for fuel first?"

*"Commander,"* Mendez interrupted, having overhead their conversation through Cameron's open mic, *"I offered him a chance to fuel up before he left. He told me he had plenty."*

"That is odd," Cameron mumbled, her eyes narrowing in suspicion. "Keep a close track on him, Kaylah."

"Aye, sir."


"So the emitters are not multipurpose after all?" Vladimir asked, seeming somewhat confused.

"No, they are not," Deliza explained. "Each emitter node can only generate a specific type of field, without variance. It's only variation is the intensity of the field."

"And by mixing the intensities of different combinations of emitters, different types of fields can be created."

"Correct."

Vladimir scratched his head. This teenage girl

had been lecturing to him for nearly an hour, and he felt no closer to understanding the fighter's shield system than he did in the beginning.

Deliza rolled her eyes, obviously losing patience with him. "That is how the system can not only change the type of shield being generated but can also alter the configuration of only certain portions of the overall field."

"You mean between absorptive and reflective, of course."

"Of course. If you wish to accelerate to superluminal velocities, then the entire field must be configured for mass reduction only. To introduce any of the other nodes would destabilize the mass reduction field."

"*Bozhe Moi*," Vladimir exclaimed. "How old are you?"

"Sixteen. Why do you ask?"

"Do all sixteen year-olds know so much about field generation and superluminal mechanics?"

"I do not believe so," she admitted, slightly embarrassed. "It is a hobby of mine."

"Hobby? The only hobby sixteen year-old girl should have is chasing sixteen year-old boys."

"I'm afraid I do not leave the farm very often," she admitted.

"That explains it," Vladimir mumbled.

"I'm sorry?" she said.

"Nothing. Now, tell me about the pulse cannons you spoke of earlier."


"Tobin is definitely headed for the spaceport," Ensign Yosef reported. "He's decelerating and losing altitude. He's preparing to land."

"Damn it," Cameron swore. "Comm, see if you can raise Tobin on the tight beam."

"Aye, sir," the communications officer responded.

"What the hell is he doing?" Cameron muttered.

"Captain," the comm officer reported, "I'm unable to establish contact with Tobin's ship. In fact, I'm no longer picking up any transmissions from Haven, sir."

"What? How can that be?"

"Either our receivers are down, or that entire moon has stopped transmitting."

"Keep trying," Cameron ordered. "And use the wide-band if you have to."

Tobin's ship rolled off the taxiway and turned into his berth. Tobin had paid particular attention to adhere to the same landing patterns as always, so as not to attract undue attention to his ship. As soon as he rolled to a stop and dropped the loading ramp on his starboard side, the black and gray armored troops came rushing out of the service building and boarded his small ship. Only being designed to seat six people at the most, the assault team was forced to stand for the short flight yet to come.

The squad leader stepped up to the cockpit door, leaning his head inside. "Get us airborne," he ordered.

Tobin nervously applied power, backing his ship out of the berth and back out onto the taxiway, turning and heading forward once more toward the nearest launch apron. Applying more power than usual, he rolled a bit faster than the maximum taxi-speed. He wanted to get this last trip over as quickly as possible.

Without even coming to a complete stop at the launch pad, Tobin applied maximum thrust to lift his small, heavily laden ship into the air, turning inland.


"Tobin is airborne again," Yosef reported.

"That was fast," Cameron commented. "Any luck raising him?" she asked her comm officer.

"No, sir."

"Something is not right," Cameron said to herself. "Kaylah, keep a close eye on Tobin, and let me know..."

"I'm going to lose him before he reaches the landing party, sir."

"What?"

"The moon's rotation, we're going to lose line of sight in just a few minutes."

"Damn it! Why didn't you tell me that before?" Cameron complained.

"I'm sorry, sir. It didn't occur to me until just now."

Cameron chastised herself for admonishing Ensign Yosef. She was a science officer, after all. She had been serving as the Aurora's only sensor officer for just a few days, and without the benefit of proper training. "That's all right, Kaylah," Cameron said, regaining her composure. "Track them as long as you can."

"Yes, sir."

"Comm, try to raise the captain, any way you can. Warn him to be ready for anything."

"I'll try, sir," the comm officer promised. "But even if he were on the air, once we lose line of sight, contact will be impossible."

"We'll reach the first touchdown point in thirty seconds," Tobin shouted from the cockpit.

The squad leader turned to face the men. "Snipers! Prepare to deploy!" The four snipers were standing in pairs at the front of each line of men standing in rows down the center of the ship. Each held tightly onto the overhead rail to steady themselves as the ship turned and banked on its landing approach.

Outside, the small ship kicked up dust and debris as it touched down on the barren ground a few hundred meters from the sinkhole which contained Tug's farm. Both the cargo door on the starboard side and the personnel door on the port side deployed as soon as the ship touched down, and the four snipers bounded down the ramps, each pair deploying in opposite directions. The snipers all ran low, heading quickly for whatever concealment they could find in their dash to take up positions along the rim of either side of the massive sinkhole.

"Can we go now?" Tobin asked the squad leader.

"Give them two minutes, then lift off and proceed to the insertion point," he ordered.

Tobin took a deep breath, rolling his eyes as he rubbed the sweat from his hands on his pant legs.


"Commander," Ensign Yosef announced. "The cargo shuttle is on approach."

Cameron had no interest in the cargo shuttle until an idea hit her. "Comm, see if you can contact the cargo shuttle."

A moment later, the comm officer reported back. "Cargo shuttle answers comms, sir."

"Then the problem is only long range. Did you check the comm array?"

"Yes, sir. Ran the diagnostics three times. It checks out."

A painful thought suddenly occurred to Cameron. "Are we being jammed somehow?" The question was directed at the communications officer.

"I don't know, sir. This console doesn't have the capability to determine the cause of the loss of signals. But if we were being jammed, wouldn't I hear static or something?"

"I'm not really sure," Cameron admitted. Their electronic countermeasures officer had been killed when his console had exploded in his face when they had rammed a Ta'Akar warship days ago. The ensign now manning communications from an auxiliary console also lacked the proper training for his current position. It was the same way throughout the ship. Key positions were being filled with anyone remotely capable. Right about now, Cameron was sorely in need of both those particular skill sets.

"Did you hear that?" Jessica asked as they strolled across the compound. She stopped dead in her tracks, trying to listen more intently.

"Hear what?" Nathan asked, stopping as well.

"I thought I heard a ship," she told him.

"I don't hear anything," Nathan said.

Jessica listened intently for a moment longer. "I could've sworn I heard a ship coming in."

"Are you sure it is safe?" Vladimir asked, standing at the top of the boarding ladder next to the cockpit.

"Of course," Deliza promised with excitement. "My father and I have been working on this for years. We have powered up the reactors many times. It is completely safe, I assure you." Deliza opened a small access panel on the underside of the ship, revealing externally mounted controls for the starboard reactor core. In a few moments, the panel came to life as the small ship began to hum almost imperceptibly. "See, I told you. The starboard reactor is now running at ten percent."

A steady beeping sound began to emanate from the cockpit next to Vladimir. He leaned down to locate the source of the alert, and found a large red lamp along the right side of the forward console flashing repeatedly in time with the beeping. "What is this flashing light?" he asked, unable to decipher the symbols that identified the light's meaning.

"What light?" Deliza climbed up the boarding ladder, squeezing in next to Vladimir to look for herself. "That's the proximity alert, but it should only go off when an enemy is nearby."

Vladimir froze as he noticed a distant sound. Within seconds the sound became louder—the engines of an approaching ship. "Go find your father," he told her, pushing her down the ladder.

"It's just a malfunction," she insisted.

The sound of a ship descending to land in the middle of the compound became quite evident. Vladimir recognized the sound of Tobin's whiny engines, and they were working harder than they should for an empty ship. "Go now!" he barked. "And stay within the tunnels. Do not go outside!" he added as he jumped down the ladder behind her.

# CHAPTER EIGHT

Tobin's ship came in low over the large barn at the opposite end of the sinkhole from the main house, immediately descending into the middle of the compound.

Jessica watched in surprise as Tobin's ship touched down rather quickly, without rotating first as he had done before. She had a terrible feeling that something wasn't right; she just couldn't figure out what that *something* was.

Tobin's rapid touchdown kicked up far more dust and debris than before, which told Jessica that he was heavily loaded. The dust wash from his landing thrusters forced the others down behind Tug's flatbed cargo hauler. As the engines wound down somewhat and the force of the thrust-wash subsided, they came out from behind the vehicle to greet Tobin. At the angle at which Tobin had set down, they could not see him in the cockpit.

Through the unsettled dust cloud and between the underside of Tobin's ship and the ground, Jessica could see the cargo door on the opposite side come down into its fully deployed position. She noticed movement to her far right and glanced to see Vladimir as he came charging out of the barn at the far end of the compound, his weapon in hand as he made for a good firing position to his right behind a trough of fertilizer. Instantly, alarms went off in her head as she looked back toward Tobin's ship. Peering under his ship to the far side, she could just make out the black, armor-clad feet of troops as they quickly disembarked and began charging toward either end of the ship.

Vladimir, having a clearer shot, opened fire as he dropped down behind the fertilizer trough, spraying the enemy troops with bullets that seemed to bounce harmlessly off their armor.

Jessica pushed Nathan and Jalea back behind the vehicle. "GET DOWN!" She swung her weapon up as she back stepped around the vehicle, flipping her safety off in one smooth motion as she opened fire, aiming under the aft end of Tobin's ship. Although she did not expect it to pierce the oncoming soldier's armored boots, she hoped it would make them think twice about sticking their heads around the aft end of the ship to fire on their poor defensive position.

From all four sides of the sinkhole, pinpoint energy weapons fire began to rain down on them from the snipers above. Danik's head exploded as a sniper's energy bolt struck him, spraying blood across Jessica as she dove behind the vehicle for cover. Vladimir saw that one of the snipers was directly behind them. He swung his weapon to his left and blasted away at the sniper above and behind Jessica and the others.

Jalea peeked under the vehicle and saw Danik lying motionless on the ground, face down in a pool of blood, most of his head missing. "DANIK!"

"Inside! Move it!" Jessica ordered as she scrambled to her feet. She knew Vladimir was providing the cover fire needed for them to get to safe cover. Nathan and Jalea scrambled for the door on the small transfer shack between the two nearest greenhouses, falling through the door as it swung open. Jessica scooted backwards, firing on the far ridge line behind Vladimir to keep the opposing sniper from picking him off before he could return to cover. Vladimir realized her target and log-rolled several times as he continued to fire small bursts at the sniper above Jessica as she too reached the relative safety of the nearest doorway.

Jessica continued firing to provide cover for Vladimir, who managed to crawl inside the transfer shack between the barn and the first greenhouse on his side of the sinkhole.

"What the hell is going on?!" Nathan yelled.

"It's a fucking ambush!" Jessica told him.

\* \* \*

Ensign Mendez was on edge. He wasn't sure if it was the anxiety in his XO's voice over their lack of radio contact with Tobin and the landing party. Of course, it also could have been all the *coffee on a stick* he had munched on to stay awake. Either way, he was more alert now than he had been in days.

He watched as the cargo shuttle pulled into its usual position in the Aurora's hangar bay. As her engines wound down, the workers approached to begin loading her for her next run. As the vapors from the shuttle's engines cleared and her rear cargo ramp began to deploy, he noticed something odd on her hull just beside the side hatch on her port side. There was scarring, a sort of rippling of the hull's skin, like it had been melted. Mendez remembered seeing that same pattern on the walls in the corridors on C deck, where Jessica and the late master chief had repelled the boarding party.

Suspicious, he rose to move in for a closer look, unslinging his weapon from his shoulder to hold across his chest in customary fashion as he walked. The rear loading ramp came down with a thud, attracting the ensign's gaze just in time to notice a horrified look on the face of the indentured worker nearest the ramp as he looked up into the back of the cargo shuttle. Reacting instinctively to the worker's terrified expression, Mendez immediately brought his weapon to bear.

On the far side of the hangar bay near the main doors, Sergeant Weatherly saw his comrade's sudden change in manner. He looked at the cockpit of the cargo shuttle and saw, not the rotund face of the same pilot he had seen for the last twenty-four hours, but the cold, ruthless face of military pilot dressed in a black flight suit and combat flight helmet.

Black and gray armored troops began pouring out of the back of the cargo shuttle, mowing down a handful of the defenseless indentured workers with rapid blasts from their energy weapons as the doomed workers scrambled for cover. Mendez ducked behind some crates to one side of the bay and immediately began spraying the rear loading ramp of the cargo shuttle with his close-quarters automatic weapon. Most of his rounds bouncing off their armor. After emptying his first clip, he counted only one enemy soldier that had fallen to his fire.

Sergeant Weatherly punched the alert button on the console next to the door as he charged to his left to try and circle around the cargo shuttle in the hope of setting up a crossfire between himself and Mendez. But before he could reach a decent firing position, one of the first enemy soldiers to come around the starboard side of the cargo shuttle caught Weatherly in the left shoulder with a blast from his energy weapon. The blast seared his shoulder, spinning the sergeant to his left and causing him to stumble and fall.

The soldier that had caught Weatherly with his first shot came rushing forward to finish the job. The sergeant had lost his grip on his weapon and it had slid a few meters away. Realizing he had no time to reach it, he pulled out his combat knife to defend himself. The onrushing enemy soldier had no intention of engaging in hand to hand combat and stopped, raising his weapon to finish Weatherly off from five meters away.

Suddenly, a large rolling cart used by the workers slammed into the side of the soldier, knocking him off his feet. Before the soldier could get back to his feet, Weatherly watched in amazement as the harvesting team foreman, Marcus, smashed the soldier's helmet with a large rock from the cart. Marcus struck the soldier several more times, making sure he was dead before standing tall in triumph.

"How do you like that, you son-of-a-bitch?" Marcus bellowed. Suddenly, weapons fire from more enemy soldiers struck the cart and the deck near Marcus, causing him to flinch and duck. "Oh shit!" he exclaimed, running to get behind the same cover that Weatherly was already crawling toward.

Marcus picked up Weatherly's loose weapon on his way, dropping down behind the crate next to the wounded sergeant. "Here! You dropped your gun!" Marcus said, handing the weapon back to Weatherly.

"Thanks," the sergeant said, disbelief still in his eyes.

"Don't mention it," Marcus said. "Now, you gonna

kill a few more of these bastards or what?"

Weatherly smiled. "Just gimme a second."

"General alarm in the hangar bay!" the comm officer reported.

Cameron touched her comm-set, "Bridge to Mendez! What's happening down there?!"

*"We're being boarded!"* he reported, the sound of his own automatic weapon answering the sound of energy weapons discharge. *"They came out of the cargo shuttle!"*

"Sound general quarters! All hands, prepare to repel boarders in the hangar bay!"

The comm officer immediately sounded the ship-wide alert as ordered, the lighting on the bridge immediately taking on a reddish hue.

Doctor Sorenson appeared from the starboard entrance, making way to her station, now designated *jump control.*

"Abby," Cameron called out, "get the drive ready to jump. We may need to exit in a hurry."

"Understood," the doctor responded.

"Mendez," Cameron called over the comms, "talk to me."

Two crewmen, armed with assault rifles, poked their heads through the main doors. The first one got caught in the shoulder by an energy bolt and was knocked back. The second crewman got the message and ducked back behind the hatch frame.

"Bridge, tell them to come in on the catwalks! They'll be able to pick them off from above!"

Mendez peeked over his cover and took a few

more shots at the enemy positions. He could see Sergeant Weatherly's foot sticking out from behind the crate on the far side of the bay, and thought he saw movement. "Sarge," he called over the comms, "you still with us?"

Sergeant Weatherly sat on the deck, his back against the crate, as he grimaced in agony at the smoking wound on his shoulder. He could feel the heat from the burned flesh as it radiated against his face. "Yeah! I'm still here," he answered over the comms.

"How bad are you hit?"

"Oh not bad. Just my fucking shoulder is on fire! That's all."

"You still in the fight?"

"Hell yeah," he answered, dragging himself to his knees and turning to face the fight.

"Can you see the starboard catwalk access ladders from your position?"

The sergeant looked over the top of the crate providing his cover. He could see both ladders on the opposite side of the cargo shuttle from where Ensign Mendez was firing. "Yeah, I can see them both."

"Good. Our people are gonna come bustin' out onto those catwalks at any moment. So don't let any of those fuckers up those ladders. Understood?"

"You got it," the sergeant answered, as he raised his weapon and opened fire on the first enemy combatant trying to ascend the catwalk ladder. Several of his rounds bounced off the trooper's armor, but one of them found a weakness in the knee joint, sending the enemy soldier falling to the deck in agony.

"Aim for their joints," the sergeant called over

the comms.

* * *

Jessica peeked around the edge of the doorway, quickly ducking back behind the heavy frame as a focused energy bolt from a sniper blasted a chunk out of the door frame, sending splinters flying in all directions.

"Fuck!" she swore, the smoke from the sizzled door frame burning her eyes. "They've got snipers up on all four sides. Vlad is laying down fire and forcing the ones on the ground to move into the buildings along the far side." She peeked out through the door again, drawing another shot from the sniper. "Shit! We can't do anything with those damned snipers up there!"

Suddenly, the side door from the neighboring greenhouse into the shack they were hiding in burst open. Jessica spun around to open fire but caught herself just in time when she saw the terrified face of Tug's oldest daughter, Deliza, standing in the doorway, frozen with fear.

"Get down!" Jessica yelled at the girl, just as another shot from the sniper shattered the window glass, narrowly missing the girl as she ducked, a scream jumping from her throat. Jessica took the opportunity to swing her weapon around the edge of the door and pop off a burst of fire at the sniper's position, just to let him know that they would fight back.

"Who are they?" Nathan asked no one in particular.

"I don't recognize their uniforms," Jessica said, "but whoever they are, they're not amateurs. That's

175

for sure."

"They are Ta'Akar assault troops," Jalea told them, "highly trained for such actions."

"I have to get to my father!" Deliza cried.

"You keep going through those greenhouses and one of those snipers will pick you off for sure," Jessica warned.

"Then we must wait?" Deliza asked.

"We can't wait," Jessica insisted. "This is probably just the first wave. They've probably got reinforcements on the way."

"My father will activate the shield."

"The emitters!" Nathan realized.

"I don't think so, honey," Jessica told her, as she peeked out the door and saw several troops making their way around the side of the main house. Tug and Ranni were firing madly through the windows but were unable to prevent the troops from advancing.

Jessica turned back to face the girl. "Where are the shield controls?"

"In the reactor shack, in the corner," she said, pointing toward the far door on the other side of the shack that led into the next greenhouse."

"Straight that way?" Jessica asked.

"Yes, all the way to the end."

Jessica peeked back out the door. The troops were getting into position to take the main house.

"They're getting ready to charge the main house. Tug and his wife are trying to hold them off." Jessica thought for a moment, the sound of weapons fire being exchanged about the main house in the distance. "Okay, new plan. I'll activate the shields. That'll get the snipers off our backs. With most of the troops headed for the main house, you guys might be able to take the ship."

"What about you?" Nathan asked.

"If I'm not back in five minutes, then I'm not comin' back."

"Jess..."

"You wanna go?" She didn't wait for a response, bolting across the room and crashing through the door into the next greenhouse."

Jessica sprinted through the first greenhouse without a single shot being fired her way. The tables were all loaded with empty dirt trays, having been freshly harvested, which meant there was little to no concealment offered. As she burst into the next transfer shack, she knew it was unlikely she'd make it so easily through the next greenhouse.

But that didn't slow her down. She charged through the shack and into the next greenhouse. This time, however, she was met with rapid sniper fire that shattered the glass windows, sending shards flying in all directions. She stumbled slightly and then fell to the deck, scrambling the last few meters on hands and knees until she was through the next door.


"Jesus!" Nathan exclaimed. "She's taking fire." He poked his weapon around the door frame and opened up on the far ridge line, hoping to force the sniper to duck for cover, but his shots were too wide of his target to have the desired effect. He peeked out the door toward the main house only to see one soldier break out in a run between the main house and Tobin's ship, skirting around the corner of the house and heading toward the back corner of the compound.

"Jess," Nathan called out of his comm-set, "one

of them is headed your way! I think he's gonna try to cut you off!" When he got no response, he called to her again. "Jess, do you copy?!"

Jessica reached up and switched off her comms as she settled down into the darkness, tucked in behind a tall rack of watering hoses. She quieted herself and forced her heavy breathing under control as she heard the sound of the outside door in the next greenhouse opening and closing, followed by the slow, careful footsteps of an armored assault trooper on the gravel floor.

Jessica pulled out her combat knife slowly and silently as the enemy drew closer to the door. Suddenly, the door swung open and the intruder burst into the room. The speed of his entry nearly startled Jessica, and it took all her nerve to control her reaction.

The soldier immediately checked behind the door but found no one. He searched the small, dark room, quickly eyed the rack of hoses in the darkened corner, and approached slowly. He pushed his weapon muzzle forward to part the hoses.

*What a dumbass*, she thought as she pushed the rack forward, causing it to fall over onto the intruder. His weapon discharged in a knee-jerk reaction, its energy blast grazing the left side of her hip as the hoses and the rack spilled forward, burying the trooper under the heavy hoses.

Screaming in pain and anger, Jessica lunged forward on top of the pile of hoses covering the enemy, pushing his weapon up and away from her as she lay atop him. Pinned on his back by the hoses and Jessica, unable to bring his weapon to bear, the soldier reached up with his left arm and grabbed a handful of Jessica's hair, pulling her head straight back.

Jessica screamed in pain as her head was pulled backward, partially lifting her up from her position on top of the soldier. She swung her right arm under his left, stabbing wildly at his chest plate. Suddenly, one of her thrusts caused the knife to deflect slightly toward her opponents chin. The knife tip slid up his chest plate and found the gap between the plate and the lower edge of his helmet's face plate. As she felt the slight advancement of her blade, she twisted her body to her right to add downward force to the blade, and it slid into her opponent's throat, bringing forth a sickening gurgling sound as his blood rushed into his trachea.

Her attacker immediately released his grip on her hair as he choked on his own blood, trying desperately to breathe. She fell forward, continuing her thrust with all her weight now behind her knife, as it chipped his cervical vertebra, sliding between them and severing his spinal cord.

His body went limp and the gurgling subsided. She sat upright, straddling her now dead opponent. She reached for the wound on her left hip, wincing in pain at her own touch. "You shot me!" she exclaimed, as she punched his face plate with her right hand. "And you pulled my hair, too!" She punched his face again. Wincing in pain, she checked her wound again. "That better not leave a scar, asshole." She withdrew her knife from his neck and had an idea.

\* \* \*

On the port catwalk of the hangar bay, three

crewmen began firing down into the group of enemy soldiers. Most of their rounds were deflected by the enemy's black armor. However, the continuous barrage of fire eventually proved to be too much for them as they began falling one by one. The soldiers scrambled for cover, but were met on either side by Weatherly to forward and Mendez to aft.

Less than a minute later, the few surviving members of the boarding party surrendered, dropping their weapons and raising up their hands. Mendez immediately rushed forward, barking at the enemy to drop to their knees as several more armed crewmen rushed in from different hatches.

"Commander," Kaylah called from the sensor station, "there's another ship trying to land."

"Where?"

"On our flight deck, sir!"

"What? Where the hell did it come from?"

"I don't know, sir. It came out of nowhere."

Outside the Aurora, an unmarked ship came in low over the drive section of the ship as it approached the flight deck.

*"Open the outer door!"* Josh, the harvester pilot, called out over the comm channel! *"I'll cut him off!"*

Cameron nearly jumped to the tactical display just in time to see the track of the harvester as it came speeding toward the Aurora from the starboard side of her stern on a collision course with the unknown approaching ship. Cameron quickly activated the transfer airlock's outer door.

The little harvester slid in under the unmarked ship, positioning himself between it and the Aurora, forcing the unmarked ship to pull up sharply at the last moment. The unmarked ship was unable to pull up enough, and it slammed into the hull just above the bay opening to the flight deck as the harvester entered the outer bay just below the unmarked ship's point of impact. The unmarked ship crumpled and flipped as its momentum caused it to slide up the hull before it spilled out over the top, chunks of it flying away as it continued to tumble out of control and break apart.

*"Whoo-hoo!"* Josh cried out. *"I never flinch!"*

"Oh my God. He'll never stop in time," Cameron declared as she watched him approach on the flight deck monitoring display. He was coming in nearly four times the normal landing speed, and he had all his thrusters burning at maximum to try and slow down before he traversed the transfer bay and slammed into the inner bay door. Cameron watched, grimacing even more intensely as she watched the harvester hurtle toward the inner doors. Suddenly he killed his thrusters and spun his little ship around, firing his main engines at full power. The harvester finally came to a stop less than a meter from the inner door. He killed his engines.

"Oh my God! You did it!" Cameron shouted, unaware that her mic was open.

*"Of course I did it, love!"* he answered as he spun his ship back around, dropped his gear and

settled onto the deck. *"Sorry I scorched your doors, though."* Cameron quickly keyed off her mic, slightly embarrassed at her outburst. *"You gonna let me in or what?"*

"Commander, hangar bay reports all secure," the comm officer reported.

Cameron took a deep breath and sighed. "Tell me that guy doesn't remind you of someone," she said as she started closing the outer bay door.

"Commander," Kaylah said, "that contact is back. It just came out from behind the gas giant."

Cameron had another sinking feeling. "Let me guess." Cameron muttered.

"Transferring track to tactical."

Cameron looked at the tactical display, watching the ship ID display as it searched for a match. Within seconds, the ID system displayed the specs for a Ta'Akar cruiser, just like the one they had faced on their way out of the asteroid field a few days ago. "Tell Mendez to get his ass up here," she ordered as she left the tactical station and made her way to the helm, "I need him at tactical. Call all hands to battle stations," she added. "We're leaving the rings."

\* \* \*

The sniper peered into his electronic sighting system, studying the little screen that showed a close-up view of the distant greenhouse. He spotted the helmeted head and armored shoulders of one of his comrades as he made his way through the greenhouse back the way he had come a few minutes earlier, in a standard tactical crouch so as to maintain a low target profile. It was an unnecessary effort that the older, more experienced sniper found amusing, attributing the extra caution to the inexperience of many of the newer members of the assault team. Satisfied that his teammate had dealt with the threat in that vicinity, the sniper continued his search for targets of opportunity.

After entering the reactor shack, Jessica removed the helmet she had taken from the soldier she had killed minutes earlier. "Jesus! Do these guys ever clean their gear?" she cursed as she tossed the helmet aside and removed the shoulder armor.

She looked around the dimly lit room until she located the target of her search—the shield control panel. There were four rows of toggle switches, about a dozen or so in each row. At one side there was a rocker switch and a lever. Unfortunately, they were all marked in a language that she did not understand.

"When in doubt, turn them all on." She quickly flipped all the toggle switches up and depressed the rocker switch. All of the little green lights above each toggle switch lit up. "So far so good," she said as she grabbed the lever and moved it all the way over. One of the large metal boxes in the room began to hum loudly, sending shivers up her spine. "Whoa. I hope it's supposed to do that." A moment later, the red light above the lever turned green, and she heard a strange whistling hum coming from outside. She moved over to the outside door of the shack and peeked out. Above the sinkhole, there was a shimmering glow of slightly opaque white with little specks dancing about. "So that's what a shield looks like, huh?" She looked over at the main farm house, not more than ten meters away. She could see soldiers about to enter the back of the house, obviously hoping to get the drop on Tug and his wife who were still firing on the troops near Tobin's ship. To her right, she could see Tobin through his cockpit windows, a nervous grin on his gaunt face as he watched the assault from the safety of his ship. "I knew we couldn't trust that skinny little fucker," she mumbled to herself, as she turned her comm-set back on.

"They're coming around to your side!" Ranni warned.

Tug looked out the broken window in front of him and saw two black and gray soldiers running for cover. He opened up on them, managing to kill the second one but missing the first when his battery pack gave out.

"Mine is dead!" he hollered.

"Take mine!" Ranni ordered, tossing her weapon to him as she turned to run toward the kitchen. "I've got another one in the kitchen!"

Suddenly, the kitchen door swung open and two red bolts of energy burst forth, striking Ranni in the chest, knocking her backwards and killing her instantly.

"RANNI!" Tug screamed as he ran to her. He dropped to his knees at her side, clutching her still smoldering and lifeless body as two soldiers stormed into the room from the kitchen door and grabbed him, wrestling away his weapon and holding him face down to the floor. They were followed by their squad leader, who strode confidently in, full of swagger. "Pick him up," he ordered.

"What was that?" Nathan asked when he heard the hum from outside.

"She did it," Jalea announced as she headed out the door. "She got the shield up."

"Wait! Where the hell are you going?" Nathan watched as she ran out across the compound, stopping momentarily at the vehicle. "Is she crazy?"

Jalea sprinted the remaining distance from the vehicle to the back of Tobin's ship.

Nathan struggled with his fear as he tried to decide what to do. He didn't know what Jalea was up to, but he was pretty sure it was a better plan than sitting on his ass waiting to get shot. At least with the overhead shield active, the snipers couldn't pick them off.

Nathan knew the shield might not last, and his fear of dying doing nothing quickly overcame his fear of dying doing something. "Stay here!" he instructed Deliza as he exited the shack in pursuit of Jalea— who by now had already circled around the aft end of Tobin's ship.

Jalea peeked around the engine cowling of Tobin's ship. His engines were still idling, and while in such close proximity, the noise was almost deafening. After seeing that there were no soldiers in sight, she moved around and made her way quickly and quietly up the cargo ramp into Tobin's small ship.

She stopped at the top of the ramp to peek inside toward the cockpit. Seeing only Tobin, she strode calmly into the ship and headed forward toward the cockpit, her weapon held down at her side.

Tobin was happily enjoying his view of the capture of Tug through the front windows of the main house when he sensed someone's presence and spun around. "Jalea," he said, his expression suddenly becoming anxious, "I can explain..."

"A little early, aren't you?" Jalea asked coldly as she raised her weapon.

Tobin's eyes widened. "Wait. We had a deal..."

Jalea fired a single shot, striking Tobin in the head, turning his skull into a mound of burnt skin, hair, and bone that slumped forward against the console as it smoldered.

Nathan came charging up the ramp a moment later, his weapon held ready. He came to a sudden stop, repulsed by the sight and smell of Tobin's smoldering head.

"What happened?"

"He was working with the Ta'Akar," she exclaimed.

Nathan was furious. "I thought you said we could trust him!"

"I said we had used his services many times in the past," she corrected. "I never said I trusted him."

"But..."

"Apparently, the Ta'Akar offered him greater payment than we did," she explained as she turned to exit.

"How the hell are we going to fly this ship?"

"I will fly it."

"Oh, so now you're a pilot as well?" he asked as he followed her.


Jessica slowly opened the back door to the main house and crept inside the storm porch. As she carefully closed the door, she noticed Tug's youngest girl hiding in a corner, huddled down low. Jessica smiled at her, and held one finger up to her pursed lips, gesturing for her to stay quiet. The little girl nodded agreement. Jessica made a goofy face at the girl to ease her tension but only got the slightest of smiles. Jessica continued on, hoping the little girl would be smart enough to stay hidden.

She continued through the next door into the kitchen, where she could hear the conversations of the soldiers who apparently had already captured Tug and his wife.

*"Do you know what they will say when we bring him in, alive no less?"* the voice came from the living room.

Jessica moved across the kitchen, coming to stop against the cabinets along the living room wall just beside the door.

*"We'll all be promoted at the very least! We may even be decorated by Caius himself!"*

*"Sir,"* another voice spoke, *"one of our snipers reports that two targets have entered the ship, and they've lost contact with Tobin."*

*"Oh no! I will not have this moment taken from me,"* the squad leader cursed. *"Bring him!"*

Jessica peeked through the crack in the door and saw them drag Tug out the front door of the house. She pushed the door open just enough to see Ranni lying dead on the floor of the living room with no one else in the room.

*"Is anybody on comms?"* Vladimir's voice came across Jessica's comm-set.

"Vlad, is that you?" Jessica whispered.

*"Yes, Jessica, I am here. Where are you?"*

"Main house, in the kitchen. Where are you?"

*"In a transfer shack to your left, just in front of the house."*

The two soldiers dragged Tug out onto the front porch, stopping just short of the front edge. Their squad leader stood directly behind Tug, holding his handgun at the back of Tug's head.

"You! In the ship!" the squad leader yelled. "Come out or we kill him!"


"Can you see them?" Jessica asked Vladimir.

"*Yes. There are three. One of them is the squad leader, I believe. They have Tug. They are holding him in front of them, on his knees. The leader has a gun to Tug's head.*"

"Where's Nathan?"

"*He is in Tobin's ship with Jalea. They are standing in the cargo doorway.*"

"Does he have his comm-set on?"

"*Yes, surprisingly.*"

"*I heard that,*" Nathan chimed in.

"You guys take out Tobin?" Jessica asked.

"*Yeah, Jalea did the honors,*" Nathan answered.

"Nice," Jessica said. "Vlad, how good a shot are you?"

"*Very good.*"

"Think you can take out the guy nearest you with a head shot?"

"*No problem.*"


The squad leader looked around as he waited. "I said come out or I will kill this man here and now!"


"Nathan, how about you? Think you can take out the one on the right with a head shot?"

*"My right or your right?"*

"My right, your left. Can you do it?"

*"Uh, I don't know,"* Nathan admitted.

"You did qualify, didn't you?"

*"Of course,"* Nathan defended. *"And I scored quite well, I might add. I've just never had to kill anyone before."*

"Well, there's a first time for everything, skipper. You gonna step up or what?" There was no answer. "Nathan?"

*"Yeah, yeah, I'm in."*

"Okay. Step out slowly. And both of you keep your weapons up and your safeties off. Let's not make this anymore difficult than we have to."


"We're coming out!" Jalea yelled from the ship.

The squad leader smiled, confident that his bluff would work. Jalea was the first out, her handgun held high, pointed at the soldiers. Nathan was next, his automatic close-quarters weapon held high and tight against his shoulder, aimed at his assigned target, the soldier on the left. "What's our signal to shoot?" Nathan whispered.

*"My count guys. On three. Repeat, on three."*

"Much better," the squad leader said. "Now lower your weapons."

*"One,"* Jessica started calmly.

"That would be unwise on our part," Jalea responded.

*"Two."*

"Not doing so would be equally unwise," the squad leader argued. "Lower them, or he dies now."

*"Three."*

All three shots rang out simultaneously. Jessica's

round entered the back of the squad leader's head, passed through his brain, and came out the front, bringing most of his face with it. Vladimir's shot entered his target in the neck, just below the jaw under his helmet line, severing his carotid artery before it exploded his cervical vertebrae, spewing blood, tissue, and bone fragments all over Tug and the squad leader standing behind him. Nathan's shot, much to his own surprise, entered dead in the center of his targets face shield, shattering the bridge of his nose as it entered his brain, passed through, and exploded the back side of his helmet, which was not designed to protect against objects trying to get out. All three soldiers dropped to the porch in dead heaps, the squad leader most dramatically as his lifeless body tumbled forward over the still kneeling farmer.

The compound became eerily still, the only sounds being the idling engines of Tobin's ship and the hum of the overhead shield. To that was soon added the sound of Deliza's cries as she ran across the compound to be by her father's side, despite the blood and bodies.

"*Are we clear?*" Jessica's voice asked over Nathan's comm-set. "*Nathan,*" she repeated, "*are we clear?*" Nathan lowered his weapon as Deliza fell into Tug's arms, weeping.

"Yeah, we're clear," Nathan answered. "All three targets are down. Tug's fine."

Jalea placed her hand on Nathan's shoulder as she holstered her weapon. "The best of men are sometimes called upon to do the worst of things," she told him before she walked away to join Tug and Deliza.

Nathan watched her walk to the porch, where she

met Jessica and took Tug's youngest daughter into her arms. Nathan could see the anguish in Tug's face and knew that his wife had not survived.

Vladimir walked past the bodies, taking note of their wounds as he passed them on his way to Nathan. "Nice shot, Nathan. To be honest, I did not think you had it in you."

"Neither did I," he admitted.

Suddenly, there was a loud *crack* that caused the ground to shake and the overhead shield to flash a blinding yellow-white. Nathan and the others instinctively ducked, as if they were expecting the very sky to come crashing down upon them. The noise came again and again, each time nearly knocking them off their feet as the blinding flashes repeated above them.

Another ship, dark gray with black trim and no markings, flew over their heads less than one hundred meters above them as it continued bombarding them from above.

"They're trying to drain the shields!" Vladimir yelled above the din.

"They cannot," Tug assured them as he got to his feet. "They can fire a thousand times; it will not weaken."

The enemy ship, satisfied that no one was returning fire, began to hover a hundred meters above the shield as it continued its bombardment.

"Maybe not," Nathan said, "but as long as that ship is up there, we're not getting out of here either!"

The ship, realizing the futility of its efforts to break the shield, turned its fire toward the edges of the sinkhole, pounding away at the ground. The walls of the sinkhole shook violently with each blast. Soon, large chunks began to shake free, falling onto the greenhouses below and shattering their glass roofs.

"What are they doing?" Nathan asked.

"They're trying to collapse the walls!" Jessica cried out.

"If they collapse the right sections, they will take out some of the emitters!" Tug warned. "When enough of them are gone, the shield will lose its integrity and collapse!"

"We've got to get out of here!" Nathan ordered. "Everyone into the ship!"

"That ship will blast us out of the air the minute we take off!" Jessica objected.

"On the ground we've got zero chance! Up there, well, it's better than nothing!" he pleaded.

"All right, you heard the captain! Everybody on board!" Jessica barked.

* * *

"We're entering orbit around Haven now," Cameron reported from the helm. "How far behind us is that warship?"

"By the time we come back around Haven, she'll have guns on us," Ensign Mendez advised from the tactical station.

"Comm, tell the surviving workers that if they want to return to Haven before we depart, they'd better do it quick."

"Yes, sir," the comm officer reported.

"Kaylah, any sign of Tobin's ship?"

"No, sir, but we're still a few minutes from line of sight with the landing party's last known position."

"Find them for me, Kaylah," Cameron ordered. "And comm, keep trying to hail them. Don't be afraid to use the wide-band."

# CHAPTER NINE

Nathan dropped into the seat to the left of Jalea in the cockpit of Tobin's ship.

"The walls are starting to come down!" Jessica yelled from the cargo door as she pushed Tobin's corpse out of the hatch.

Nathan looked out the windows and saw the wall to the left of him, toward the back corner of the ship, come apart under the force of the continuous barrage. Finally, a large section of it came crashing down, taking three emitters with it. The shield overhead flickered several times.

"It's failing!" Tug yelled.

Another section of the wall, on the same side but nearer them, also collapsed, burying the greenhouse below. The shields flickered a few more times then disappeared altogether.

"Get us in the air!" Nathan ordered.

Jalea pushed the lift throttles forward and the ship began to slowly rise. Rocks and debris fell off the crumbling walls and bounced off the ground, striking the side of the ship. They were only eight meters off the ground when the first salvo struck them in the aft port thrust pod. Their tail dropped sharply and the ship began to roll over to port.

"Compensate!" Nathan yelled.

Jalea tried to compensate by increasing the lift on the port side, but the thrust pod was damaged and not responding. Alarms began to sound as the ship rolled completely over, causing her still firing lift thrusters to drive her hard, upside down, into the ground. A moment later, they all found themselves lying on the ceiling of the ship, alarms whooping away and the acrid smell of leaking propellant filling their nostrils.

Nathan shook his head, spitting dirt from his mouth. All the windows on his side of the cockpit had been shattered by the force of impact, and dirt had flown into the cockpit as they rolled over. Sections of the overhead control panel, which he was now laying on top of, dug into his side as he tried to get his feet under him. "Jalea!" he yelled. She wasn't moving. "Jalea, are you okay?" She began to stir, her consciousness returning. "Come on, we've gotta get outta here!"

Nathan grabbed Jalea and pulled her toward him. "Come on, come on," he urged pushing her out in between the partitions toward the back of the ship. "Let's go! Everybody out!"

Vladimir slid out of the ship, face first down onto the dirt two meters below. The ship was upside down, slightly on its starboard side. Dust and smoke were everywhere, making it hard to see more than a few feet in front of him. Alarms continued to warble and beep.

"Vlad," Jessica called from above, "catch her!" Vladimir extended his arms just in time to catch Tug's youngest daughter as she fell from the ship. He set her down next to him.

"Do not move, little one," he instructed. He reached up and grabbed Deliza by the waist as she tried to climb down from the ship, helping her down to the ground. "Grab your sister's hand and do not let go, no matter what. And stay by my side!" Deliza nodded instant agreement.

Nathan jumped down to the ground, followed by Jalea. Suddenly, pinpoint blasts of energy from sniper fire started striking the ship and the ground around them. The dust and smoke were still too thick to see very far, so the snipers were taking blind shots in the hopes of hitting something or someone.

"Son-of-a-bitch!" Nathan swore. "We've gotta get to cover!" Nathan spun around as shots struck the dirt on either side of him. He tried to get his bearings. In the haze, he could barely make out the shape of the main house. "Over there!" he shouted. "Head for the house!"

Jalea ran for the house. Vladimir scooped up the little girl, grabbed Deliza's arm, and followed.

"Jess, let's go!" Nathan ordered.

"Tug is hung up on something!" she yelled from inside the ship.

Nathan could hear the sound of the enemy ship that had shot them down before they could get airborne as it turned and headed back toward them. "They're comin' back around, Jess! You gotta get out now!"

Jessica struggled to free Tug's leg, which was pinned between a twisted section of the bench seat and the wall. Somehow, as the ship had rolled over, the bench had pulled free. Tug's leg had slid in between the bench and the wall, and when the ship came down, the bench had folded back and had trapped his leg between it and the bulkhead.

"Leave me!" Tug begged her.

"Oh, don't be so fucking dramatic!" she scolded.

"Come on, Jess!" Nathan called from outside.

"Go, Nathan! We'll catch up in a minute!"

"God damn it, Jess!" Nathan swore as he departed, running for the cover of the house.

The ship began to shake with increasing violence as the salvos from the approaching enemy ship grew closer with each strike. Finally, the last two energy bolts struck the ship, chopping its rear section clean off. The shearing force rocked the ship and freed Tug's leg. Falling free of his entrapment, he landed on top of Jessica as they both fell against the far side of the upside down ship.

"Well how about that?" Tug exclaimed.

Suddenly, flames ignited from the leaking fuel lines. Within seconds, the flames blocked the starboard cargo hatch, which had been their intended route of egress.

"This thing's gonna blow!" Jessica exclaimed as she tried in vain to find a way past the flames.

Nathan finally reached the front steps of the porch when the sound of an explosion came from behind him. A searing hot shock wave launched him forward. He went crashing through the partially opened front door.

"Nathan, are you all right?!" Vladimir shouted as he ran to help his friend to his feet.

"Oh my God!" Nathan exclaimed as he realized what had happened. He spun around and tried to go back out the front door. "JESS!" Another explosion rocked the house, sending hundreds of small pieces of flaming debris showering in all directions. Nathan had to brush some of the burning fuel from his own clothing to avoid going up in flames himself. He turned to Vladimir, "Jessica and Tug! They were still in there!"

Vladimir grabbed Nathan and pulled him inside. "Come, my friend. There is nothing more you can do for them."

\* \* \*

Kaylah zoomed in on the landing party's last reported location. As the small farm had just come over the horizon on the moon below, her observation angle was quite steep, making it difficult to see much of the compound contained within the sinkhole. But there was no doubt about what she did see—a large explosion followed by flame and smoke.

"Commander, something is happening at the landing party's last reported location. There's been an explosion," Kaylah reported.

"Can you see the landing party?"

"No, sir, there's too much smoke, and our angle is still too steep to get a good overhead." Kaylah noticed movement above the smoke. "Standby. There's something else." She quickly changed sensor mode from visual to radar, allowing her to clearly track a small ship circling the sinkhole. "It's a ship, sir. Same size and configuration as the one that tried to land on us earlier."

Cameron didn't like the sound of Ensign Yosef's report. "Any sign of Tobin's ship?"

"I'm not sure, sir." Kaylah reset her sensors back to visual mode and applied various filters to try and discern the shape of the burning object. After keying in additional commands, information detailing the chemical properties of the smoke she was seeing began to list on one of her side screens. "I'm pretty sure that's Tobin's ship that's burning. Its shape is very similar, but there's no way to be sure. At least not until we get closer."

"Any luck contacting them over comms?" she asked the communications officer.

"No, sir. And I'm trying all modes, even open channels on the wide-band."

"Damn it," Cameron swore. "We've got less than half an hour to get them back, or we're going to have to leave them behind. And for all we know that *is* Tobin's ship burning down there. We need another ship."

A smile formed on the face of Ensign Mendez as he stood at the tactical station. "Last I looked, there were two of them in the hangar bay."

"Contact those ships," she instructed the comm officer. "See if one of them is willing to fetch the landing party."

"You think they'll do it?" Mendez asked. "I mean, willingly?"

"Maybe, if we pay them enough," Cameron mumbled.

"Commander," the comm officer said, "the only one answering is the harvester pilot. Shall I transfer him to your comm-set?"

"Sure," Cameron answered. She was feeling a bit overwhelmed by the constantly changing circumstances. It felt like every time she came up with a plan, something happened, forcing her to change it. For someone who always liked to have a solid plan to follow, it was frustrating.

A moment later, Josh's voice came over Cameron's comm-set. *"What can I do for ya, love?"*

Cameron rolled her eyes at the cocky pilot's attitude. "We've got people on the surface, presumably with no way back up. Think one of your shuttles could go down and get them, really quickly?"

*"How quick we talking?"*

"Thirty minutes, max."

*"I'm guessing your hurry has something to do with that Ta'Akar battle cruiser heading our way."*

"That would be a good guess."

*"Sorry, but the second shuttle's all shot up, and it's blocking the first one from launching. Maybe if we had more time to move it..."*

"What about your ship?" Cameron interrupted. "Can you still launch?"

*"Sure, but how many people we talking about? I'm made for scooping up rocks, not hauling passengers."*

"Four or five."

*"Yeah, I guess I can squeeze them in, so long as they don't mind a bumpy ride. This thing's not built for comfort, you know."*

"Great," Cameron exclaimed. "But how much is it going to cost me?"

*"You can buy me dinner,"* Josh suggested playfully.

"I'm sure we can figure out some manner of payment. But I think I should warn you, there may be some trouble at the pickup point."

*"Then make it two dinners!"*

"How soon can you depart?" she asked, ignoring his solicitations.

*"I'll be wheels up in a few minutes, love. Just send me their coordinates."*

"Thanks, Josh," she told him, "and good luck."


The harvester began quickly backing out of the hangar bay, headed for the transfer airlock at a rate slightly faster than normal. The helmeted pilot, his faceplate still hiding his facial features, constantly rotated his head from side to side as well as looking down at his consoles as he tried to keep from hitting anything in the chaotic aftermath of the earlier boarding attempt.

"Any luck contacting them?" Cameron asked the comm officer.

"No, sir. I'm pretty sure someone is jamming communications on the surface."

"The harvester is rolling onto the flight deck now, Commander," Ensign Mendez reported from the tactical station.

"Warn the pilot about the comm jamming going on down there," she ordered Mendez.

The harvester continued to roll quickly backward as it came out of the transfer airlock and onto the open flight deck. It immediately applied slight upward thrust, its gear retracting as soon as it left the deck. Another short burst shooting forward from braking thrusters embedded in the harvester's nose caused it to float back away from the ship more quickly. Applying side thrust, the little ship quickly slid to the right, clearing the ship just before the large drive section was about to slam into it from behind. As it cleared the side of the ship, it snap-rolled to the right and swung its nose down, firing its main engines at full thrust as it accelerated quickly away from the Aurora on its journey to the moon below.

"The harvester's away," Mendez chuckled. "Damn that guy..."

"Flies like a nut," Cameron finished. "Yeah, I know. But that nut is the only hope they've got right now."

\* \* \*

Nathan continued looking out the broken front window of the main house. The air outside was still thick with black and gray smoke from the burning wreckage of Tobin's ship, which was less than a dozen meters away. Thankfully, there had been no more shots fired at them by the snipers since they had made it inside the house. "What the hell are they waiting for?"

Deliza sat in the corner, holding her younger sister in her lap, keeping her little head against her chest to keep her from staring at her mother's corpse on the living room floor. Jalea knelt beside them, trying to calm the child.

"Reinforcements," Vladimir suggested.

"Yes," Jalea agreed, rising from the girls to move back toward the others at the windows. "They must be coming from elsewhere—a ship in orbit, perhaps—or they'd already be upon us."

Nathan looked outside again, trying to see the snipers through the smoke. "If we could just get past those snipers, we might be able to make our way back to town on foot, maybe find another way off this moon and back to the ship."

"I expect there is a Ta'Akar ship nearby," Jalea advised him. "If so..."

"Then the Aurora's got her own problems to deal with," Nathan surmised. "Hell, they've probably already jumped away."

"You worry too much, Nathan," Vladimir said.

"They will come for us. You will see."

"God, I hope you're right."

Suddenly, the snipers began firing through the windows. Blasts of energy broke through the remaining glass, slamming into floors and furniture, sending splinters flying in all directions and charring everything they struck. Jalea grabbed the girls, dragging them down to the floor and pushing them into the corner tucked in behind a cabinet.

Vladimir scrambled on his hands and knees to the side window and began firing blindly toward the ridge line with his handgun, hoping he'd get lucky and hit one of the snipers. Following his friend's example, Nathan scrambled to the opposite side and did the same.

Moments later, the shuttle began firing its pulse cannon at the main house. Each blast tore through the roof, passing through the upper floor and breaking through the ceiling above them. It brought a shower of debris down on top of them with every blast. The young girls screamed with each blast.

"Jesus!" Nathan yelled. He had little doubt that they were all about to be either buried in a pile of burning debris or completely vaporized.

"They're trying to drive us out into the open," Vladimir replied, "to force us to surrender!"

"By bombing the crap out of us?" Nathan asked as he continued firing wildly out the window.

One of the main beams cracked and bowed downward, bringing more debris from the ceiling above. With the following blast, the beam split completely, crashing to the floor and narrowly missing Vladimir.

"We've got to get out of here!" Nathan hollered, scrambling across the shattered living room toward the kitchen. "Through the back!"

As if the shuttle's gunner had heard him, the next few salvos impacted the back half of the house, collapsing the kitchen roof. Nathan opened the kitchen door just in time to see the ceiling come crashing down, dust and debris bouncing up into his face in the doorway, knocking him backward into the living room. "Guess not!"

Josh looked out the windshield over the nose of the harvester as it raced along less than fifteen meters above the surface of the Haven countryside. In the distance, maybe twenty kilometers in front of them, he could see the pillar of black smoke rising from the surface, spreading to the right as it rose into the sky.

"Twenty seconds out," his copilot, Loki, reported over the whine of the engines. The two of them had been flying the harvester together for nearly six months, ever since Josh had first arrived on Haven.

"Volander landing party, Harvester. Do you copy?" Josh waited a few seconds for an answer, but got none. "Guess we're gonna have to surprise them," he smiled.

Loki tightened the shoulder straps on his flight harness. Although Josh was an amazing pilot, he had a tendency to do things without warning. "You sure you wanna go in so fast, Josh?"

"This'll have to do," Josh chuckled.

As the distance closed, they could begin to make out the shape of the enemy shuttle as it circled over the sinkhole, firing its pulse cannon at targets below.

"Pulse cannons," Loki pointed out.

"I see them."

"I'm assuming you've got a plan."

Josh said nothing, only clucked like a chicken.

"Great," Loki said, grabbing the handholds on the top edges of the front and side consoles to brace himself. He knew what was coming, and he knew from experience that he'd best hold on tight.

As they rapidly closed on the enemy shuttle, it continued its slow circle, turning toward the oncoming harvester.

"Oh shit!" Loki cried.

For a brief moment, Loki was sure he could see the faces of the flight crew on the shuttle as it suddenly rolled sharply to its right to avoid colliding with the onrushing harvester. Josh immediately rolled slightly opposite the enemy ship, pulling his nose up ever so slightly to send his ship into a tight, high-G turn. "YES!" he cried out in victory. "I NEVER FLINCH!"

The enemy shuttle did not pull his nose up as he rolled, which resulted in a sudden loss of altitude bringing him below the top of the sinkhole and sending him diving toward its wall.


Inside the main house, the sound of the harvester rocketing by at high velocity shook the entire structure, knocking them off their feet. For a brief moment, they were deafened by the roar of the harvester's main drive as it blew past them at incredible speed.

"What the hell was that?" Nathan wondered as he picked himself up, noticing that the bombardment had stopped. A moment later the ground shook once more as a tremendous crash came from outside.

Nathan spun around to look out the windows. Through the smoke he could barely make out the image of the enemy shuttle as it slammed into the side of the sinkhole, falling into the greenhouse below before exploding.

"Holy shit!"

*"Volander landing party, Harvester. Do you copy?"* The voice coming over his comm-set was unfamiliar to him, but Nathan answered the hail nonetheless.

"This is Captain Scott! Who's calling?"

*"It's your ride, Captain! That sweet little commander of yours sent us to bring you home!"*

"Sweet little commander?" Vladimir wondered.

"He must be talking about Cameron," Nathan said.

"Great!" Nathan told him over the comms. "How did you take out that shuttle?"

*"No time to chitchat, Captain. I've gotta deal with a few snipers first. Get your people ready to move out! I'll be down in a minute to pick you up!"*

"Copy that!" Nathan answered.

"There's another explosion at their position!" Kaylah reported.

"Who is it?" Cameron snapped. "Is it the harvester?"

"No, sir! I show the harvester still maneuvering!" Ensign Mendez reported with excitement. "The son-of-a-bitch took him head on at max velocity!"

"Christ! He played chicken with them?"

"That guy is insane!" Mendez exclaimed.

Loki flinched as sniper rounds struck the nose of

the harvester. "They're shooting at us, Josh!"

"No shit, really?"

The harvester dipped down to no more than two meters above the ground as it reached the first sniper, who dove out of the way. A few seconds later Josh turned hard to starboard, smacking the next sniper with the thrust wash from his main drive and knocking him off the cliff into the sinkhole.

Vladimir looked out the window to try and determine why the snipers were no longer firing at them. He quickly realized the cause of their distraction when he saw the harvester come swinging around to line up with the opposite ridge line. "He's buzzing the snipers!"

On the next pass, Josh flew so low that his exhaust was lighting the sparse vegetation on fire. Loki closed his eyes as they nearly slammed into the first sniper, who dove face down hoping to avoid being hit, only to find his own armor melting to his back due to the heat of the passing harvester's exhaust. A few seconds later, there was a sickening *thud*.

"OH SHIT!" Josh yelled.

Loki opened his eyes again, only to see a red smear on the nose of the harvester that ran up onto the front windshield. "What happened?"

"I took off his fucking head!" Josh giggled.

Loki shook his head. "You're a sick little dude. You know that, don't you?"

The harvester pulled up hard until it was almost vertical, backing off on the power until it was about to stall. As it did, the ship banked over to port and dove back down, pulling up just enough to angle toward the center of the sinkhole. Within seconds they were nearly there, and Josh pulled up the nose, firing his landing thrusters at maximum burn to stop their descent. The little ship came to a hover in the middle of the compound, directly in front of the main house, spinning around to point its nose toward the front door before extending its gear and dropping the last meter to the ground.

The side hatch to the harvester popped open. Loki leaned out to wave at the landing party, signaling them to move quickly as they exited the main house and ran toward the ship. Vladimir scooped up the little girl and handed her up to Loki who pulled her into the ship. Deliza was next, followed by Jalea.

"We've gotta go back and look for Jessica!" Nathan shouted.

"There's no time!" Loki objected. "There's a warship on the way! If we're not back in ten minutes, your ship's leaving without you!"

"But she could still be alive!" Nathan argued.

"Nathan, we've got to go!" Vladimir insisted.

"No! I have to be sure!"

"Nathan, you're the captain now! Your responsibility is to your ship!" Vladimir grabbed Nathan by the collar and shoved him up the side of the harvester. "Now get in there!" Vladimir shoved Nathan up to the hatch, climbing up behind him.

There were only two seats in the small cabin behind the cockpit of the harvester, which were taken by Jalea on one side and Deliza on the other with her little sister in her lap. Nathan and Vladimir crammed themselves onto the floor, between Jalea's feet and the front bulkhead that separated the small cabin from the cockpit. Loki pulled the hatch closed and stepped over them, returning to the cockpit as he hollered, "Let's go!"

Before Loki even sat down, the harvester leapt into the air, its main drive kicking in and sending it accelerating away as its landing gear retracted.

"Message from the harvester, sir," the comm officer reported. "They're inbound with five passengers!"

"Yes!" Cameron said, a wave of relief washing over her. "What's their ETA?"

"Ten minutes, sir."

Cameron turned to Ensign Mendez at the tactical station directly behind her.

Mendez shook his head, a dour look on his face. "Eight minutes and we'll be toe-to-toe with that warship."

Cameron took a deep breath, letting it out slowly. "I don't suppose we have the torpedoes working yet?" Another look from Mendez confirmed what she already knew. "Battle stations everyone. Deploy the rail guns, point-defense mode."

"We've got company!" Loki reported as he buckled himself back into his seat. "Ta'Akar fighters on an intercept course. They'll be on us in two."

"Hang on, ladies and gentlemen!" Josh yelled over his shoulder toward the back cabin. "It's gonna get interesting!"

Vladimir raised his feet and planted them firmly against the bulkhead opposite him, on either side of Nathan, to brace himself. With his left hand, he grabbed the edge of the arm rest of the seat next to him where Deliza sat holding her younger sister in her lap. "Excuse me."

Nathan copied Vladimir's preparations, bracing himself in similar fashion as the small ship bounced and vibrated on its wild ascent.

"Enemy vessel is breaking the horizon," Mendez reported from tactical. "She'll have guns on us in thirty seconds."

Cameron looked at her flight and navigation displays. If they broke orbit now and accelerated away from the planet at maximum sub-light speeds, she could jump away without taking any fire from the incoming warship. But that would condemn the entire landing party, which she wasn't ready to do just yet. On the other hand, if she waited too long, by the time the harvester caught up to them, there was a good chance there would be little left of them to catch up to.

"Abby," Cameron hailed, "I don't suppose we could jump from orbit."

"I would not advise it," she warned.

"Yeah, why is that again?"

"The effect of the moon's gravity well could cause our arrival point to be considerably off target. Who knows where we could come out…"

"Yeah, in the middle of a sun. I got that. But how far off might Haven's gravity well make us?"

"I'm not really sure. It took us days to calculate the effects of Jupiter's gravity well on our first jump."

"Well, if you had to guess."

"I'm not sure I could. There are so many variables— like the distance of the jump, for example. And there are two gravity wells here—both the moon's and the planet's."

"But if the jump were short, say, a few million kilometers?"

Abby was suddenly deep in thought. "Give me a minute," she said as she began furiously making calculations.

"We're hit!" Loki cried out. The back of Nathan's head slammed against the wall as the aft end of the harvester suddenly shifted violently to starboard.

"It's okay! It's okay!" Josh reported. "We're still good!" Josh pulled the control stick hard over and gave it a twist with his right hand as he manipulated the main thrust throttles with his left. The harvester suddenly rolled to starboard, going into a spiraling maneuver that caused them to drop significantly below their original glide path, forcing their pursuers to adjust their attack. The maneuver was just another of a series of bizarre attempts to avoid the incoming fire from the two Ta'Akar fighters that had intercepted them shortly after takeoff.

So violently had Josh twisted the little harvester around, that Nathan had completely lost track of their course and attitude in relation to Haven. During his flight training back at the academy, he had spent several months qualifying in small tactical craft, including the Tactical Space Fighter used by the fleet. That training had included an array of evasive tactics and maneuvers, but none of that had prepared him for what they were currently experiencing. It was all that Nathan could do to keep from dry heaving.

He opened his eyes. The cabin was darker than before, lit only by the flashes of energy blasts as they streaked by them. The internal lighting had been shut down to save power for use by the harvester's limited shielding. He looked at Vladimir, who also looked a little shaken.

A grin suddenly spread across Vladimir's face. "This pilot, he is either very good, or he is very drunk!"

Nathan looked at Tug's daughters. Deliza held her little sister tightly on her lap. The child had her face buried in her sister's chest, not wanting to see any of what was going on around them.

Jalea appeared nearly as shaken as the rest of them, but continued to stare straight ahead out the front windshield, as if trying to keep track of the events transpiring outside in the vacuum of space.

The ship rocked again as another blast stuck them on the starboard side, super-heating the bulkhead that Vladimir was leaning against, drawing a Russian curse as he leaned forward abruptly to avoid serious burns to his back. Luckily, the cold of space quickly cooled the exterior, and within seconds the bulkhead was only warm to the touch.

"Bozhe Moi," he exclaimed. "The hull must not be very thick." His eyes were wide with the realization of how little material was between them and the weapons that were being repeatedly fired at them.

"There she is!" Loki announced, pointing to the right.

"She's taking fire!" Josh added.

Despite the shaking and the sparks showering down from an overhead circuit panel, Nathan somehow managed to get to his knees and crawl forward enough to peer out the forward windshield of the harvester. A few hundred kilometers in front of them was the Aurora—his ship—and it was taking fire as it waited for them to reach the relative safety of her hangar bay. It was nothing more than a speck. If it hadn't been for the explosions of energy weapons against her hull, he might not have been able to pick it out against the stars.


"Two minutes!" Mendez called over the noise of battle. He watched his tactical display as the harvester darted about, jerking to and fro as he tried to shake the fighters off his tail. "He can't evade them forever! Nobody's that lucky!"

Explosions, otherwise silent in the dead of space, reverberated through the ship. Alarms warning of stressed systems played from nearly every console on the bridge. The constant din of the bridge staff as they communicated with the rest of the crew throughout the ship during battle was almost overwhelming.

"How's it look, Abby?" Cameron asked from the helm.

"I think it'll work."

"You think?"

"It will work," she insisted. "How far do you want to jump?"

"How long does it take to calculate a normal jump, say something at least a few light years?"

"Fifteen, maybe twenty minutes."

"How long will it take you to calculate a jump thirty light minutes away from here?"

"A few minutes at the most," Abby said.

"So quick?"

"The shorter the jump, the easier it is to calculate."

"Do it," Cameron ordered.

The ship rocked as another missile got through

their weakened point-defense field.

"Damn it! I wish I could take evasive maneuvers!" But she knew she had to hold a steady course until the harvester made it safely to their flight deck.

"We just lost another turret!" Mendez reported. "We're down to eight!"

Cameron knew that there was no way they could maintain an effective point-defense field with only eight functioning rail gun turrets.

"Shit! There's a third one!" Loki announced. "Four o'clock, farther back!"

"Son-of-bitch!" Josh declared. "Who are you people?" Josh shouted over his shoulder. He was beginning to wonder who it was he and Loki had gotten mixed up with, and why the Ta'Akar wanted them so badly.

It was the first time since they had been rescued that Nathan had heard any desperation in the crazy pilot's voice. Nathan looked at Vladimir, whose own expression was as serious as he had ever seen.

"Na...an......you......py?" The voice over his comm-set was broken and barely understandable. But it was familiar. He instinctively cupped his hands over his ears, trying to isolate the voice from all the noise in the bouncing ship.

"...than, this is......ssica! D.........copy?"

"Oh my God!" Nathan mumbled. "Jess, is that you?" he called back over the comm-set. "Where are you?"

"In......ighter......hind you!"

"It's Jessica!" Nathan hollered.

"What?" Vladimir couldn't believe it.

"Chan......ourse! Hard......ight!"

"What? You're breaking up! Can you repeat?"

"Change......rse!    Co......ard......right!    Do...t... now!"

Nathan suddenly realized what was happening. "Change course! Come hard to starboard now!"

"What?" Josh asked, wondering if Nathan had lost his mind.

"DO IT!"

Josh got the message, and immediately put the little ship into a tight right turn. "How long do you want me to hold this turn?"

"The third fighter is firing on the first one!" Mendez reported, a bit confused by what he was witnessing.

"What?" Cameron was also shocked.

"Holy shit! He's gone! The first fighter is gone! The second one is breaking their pursuit! He's trying to evade the third one!"

"What the hell?" Cameron mumbled.

"Oh yeah!" Jessica cheered from the back seat of the old fighter.

Tug yanked the stick to the left and added power to his engines. "The other one's breaking off. I'm going after him."

"What the hell for?" Jessica argued. "Let's just get the hell out of here, shall we?"

"He's faking retreat," Tug insisted. "He'll try to come around and get behind us."

"How do you know?"

"That's what I would do," Tug answered calmly.

"Okay."

*"Jess, where did you come from?"* Nathan asked over the comm-set. *"Is Tug with you?"*

"Who do you think is flying this thing?" she laughed.

"Commander, the third fighter is a friendly!" the communications officer reported.

"How do you know?" Cameron challenged.

"I'm picking up traffic between it and the harvester," he told her as he transferred the signal to the loudspeakers.

*"Long story, skipper,"* Jessica's voice said over the comms. *"I'll fill you in later. Now head for the ship while we take out the other punk. And tell Cam not to leave without us!"*

"What the hell happened down there?" Cameron wondered aloud.

"They're flying into the warship's firing solution," Mendez warned. "They won't survive a hit from their big guns."

"Then let's give them some cover," Cameron said, as she cut the main engines and pulled back on the controls.

The Aurora's nose pitched up, stopping at a ninety degree angle to her flight path. Unable to maintain a firing solution for a point-defense field, the rail guns automatically stopped firing. The enemy warship, however, did not. It continued its relentless barrage.

"What the hell is she doing?" Loki asked as they watched the Aurora pitch up.

"That lady's as crazy as I am," Josh laughed.

Nathan also laughed. "She's showing them her belly," he explained. "It's the toughest part of the ship."

With no point-defense field to at least partially protect them, the Aurora was taking every shot at full force into her undersides, but it had been designed to be used for emergency aero-braking and atmospheric entry in the event of a crash landing. With three times as many layers as the rest of the ship, and much heavier structural support, Cameron hoped that the Aurora's bottom side would protect them all long enough to recover the two smaller ships and jump away. It wasn't exactly a textbook maneuver, but it was working.

The second fighter was now only fifty meters in front of them as they chased him through a tight turn to port. The enemy pilot kept varying his turn rate in a desperate effort to trick Tug into losing his target lock. However, it was to no avail, as this wasn't Tug's first dogfight.

A small puff of maneuvering thrust squirted out of the nose of the second fighter, just as it had numerous times over the last few seconds during the turn. This time, it was a bit more thrust than usual.

"You can't be that stupid," Tug mumbled.

The enemy fighter suddenly began to rapidly pitch back as it tried to do an end-over-end to bring its own guns to bear on Tug and Jessica. For a brief moment, the enemy's profile became considerably larger, giving Tug a splendid target and an easy kill. A single squeeze of the trigger on his control stick, and a red bolt of energy leapt from his cannon striking the enemy dead center, rupturing his fuel tanks and igniting a blinding explosion.

"What happened?" Jessica asked as the debris from the exploding enemy ship struck them like rain falling from the sky.

"Caius was always more interested in quantity than quality," Tug mumbled.

"What?" Jessica asked from behind.

"Nothing. Let's rejoin the others."


"Hang on, people!" Josh yelled from the cockpit. "This ain't gonna be pretty!"

"What's wrong?" Nathan asked. After the Aurora had pitched up and started blocking the incoming fire, their ride had been comparatively smooth.

"We've got a lot of damage, and a nose dive ain't exactly an ideal angle for a landing!"

Nathan looked forward between the partitions. Through the forward windshield of the cockpit, he could see the Aurora, not more than a hundred meters away and coming up fast. But since she had pitched up, their approach was now perpendicular to her length. There was no way they could change course fast enough to avoid smashing head first into her flight deck. "Oh my God."


"Tell me you're ready, Abby!" Cameron said.

"Hangar bay, prepare for crash landing!" Mendez called over the comms. "All hands brace for collision!"

"I'm ready!" Abby promised.

"Hang on, people! We're gonna have to take a few more shots to the nose!" Cameron announced.

"HA HA!" Josh screamed, his eyes widening. Nathan spun his head back to his left to look forward once more.

"She's pitching down!" Loki yelled.

"Oh I'm in love with that woman!" Josh cheered.

Nathan watched as the Aurora pitched her nose back down until it once again was pointed in the same direction as her heading. Now they had a somewhat normal approach angle, although they were still coming in fast.

"They've launched missiles!" Ensign Mendez reported. "Six inbound! All conventional! ETA thirty seconds!"

"Standby, Abby!"

Abigail moved her hand over the large round jump button that one of the technicians had permanently wired into her console now that it was the official Jump Control station. She flipped open the cover and turned the key above the button, arming it. "Standing by," she answered, her finger hovering over the button.

"Here we go!" Josh announced. He pulled his nose up hard and fired his landing thrusters. Designed to provide the lift needed for atmospheric flight, other than his mains they were the most powerful engine he had and therefore the most effective at quickly reducing their forward velocity. A quick glance to his right, Josh saw Tug doing the same thing with his old fighter as he too tried to make an emergency landing right next to them.

"Let's hope she remembered to open the outer doors this time," Josh mumbled.

As they slid in under the flight deck's canopy, they pushed their nose back down and extended their landing gear. But there was not enough time for the harvester's gear to fully extend before it hit the flight deck. The gear folded back up against the harvester's underside in twisted heaps.

Tug's fighter fared better, its gear extending more rapidly and locking just in time to touch down with considerable force. Having suffered far less damage than the harvester, Tug's fighter was able to use its braking thrusters to come to a comfortable and controlled stop.

The harvester, however, was not so lucky. It slid across the flight deck into the outer airlock bay, sparks flying as it careened off the starboard wall and skidded back out toward the center of the bay, nearly colliding with Tug's fighter.


"They're down!" Mendez reported.

"Kill main viewer," Cameron ordered. "Jump!"


A pale blue wave of light washed out from the Aurora's shield emitters. In a split second, the bluish light grew into a glowing ball that encompassed the entire ship, before it suddenly turned white and fell back in upon her, erasing the ship from local existence. It left nothing but an empty hole in space for the approaching missiles to cruise through.

"Jump completed," Abby reported no more than a second later.

"Main viewer up," Cameron ordered. "Kaylah, get a fix on our position, and then locate that warship. And let's try to reduce our emissions as much as possible. The harder it is for them to spot us, the more time we'll have to prepare for our next jump."

"Already on it, sir," Ensign Yosef reported.

"Abby, start plotting an escape jump, open space, anywhere outside of this system.

"Which direction?"

"Don't really care." Cameron turned to Mendez at tactical. "Did they make it?"

"Don't know yet, sir. The outer doors just finished closing. The transfer airlock will be repressed in two minutes."

"Very well. Good work, everyone."

"Commander?" Ensign Yosef called. "Okay, this is really weird."

"What is it?" Cameron asked tentatively. Their history of unexpected occurrences had been nearly non-stop since they had departed Earth a week ago.

"I've found the warship."

"Great. Where is it?"

"It's still on the far side of the gas giant."

"What?"

"Yes, sir. It's right where it would've been before we first detected it." Kaylah's eyes suddenly widened and her mouth hung open. "Oh my God, and there's us."

"What?" Cameron repeated more emphatically.

"Okay," Kaylah exclaimed, "this is going to take some getting used to." She turned to face Cameron.

"We're thirty-eight light minutes out from Haven, sir. We're seeing what *was*, what happened thirty-eight minutes ago. I'm seeing *us* still sitting in the rings."

"Whoa," Mendez said aloud.

Cameron smiled. "You're right. That *is* going to take some getting used to."

# CHAPTER TEN

As soon as the inner transfer airlock door rose far enough, crewmen carrying portable fire extinguishers, rescue gear, and medical bags came ducking under, pouring into the bay. Most headed straight for the harvester, knowing that it contained their landing party.

Tug's fighter, having landed without significant damage, had already pulled to one side and shutdown its engines. By the time the would-be rescuers reached him, his canopy was already open and his helmet removed.

The harvester, however, was in much worse shape. Having slammed into the deck and the wall before sliding back into the open, the poor little ship was fairly mangled and would obviously never fly again.

As rescuers ran toward the harvester, the hatch cracked open slightly. Vladimir pushed from the inside, trying to get the stuck hatch open as acrid smoke from burning circuits within the ship came seeping out of the hatchway. The rescuers quickly climbed onto the battered harvester and began prying at the hatch from the outside, but to no avail. Within seconds, another rescuer brought up a heavy powered cutting tool and quickly sliced through the hinges of the hatch, freeing it from the harvester.

With the hatch now removed, the remaining gray

smoke poured out of the harvester. Vladimir quickly tossed Tug's youngest out of the ship like a doll, into the arms of his fellow crewmen below who rushed her away from the smoldering wreckage. Deliza was next, followed by Jalea, Nathan, and Vladimir.

Hacking and coughing, Nathan immediately called to Cameron on his comm-set. "Cam! What's our status?"

*"We're safe for now, Nathan, at least for a couple of hours. Is everyone all right?"*

"Cuts and bruises mostly," Nathan answered as he turned around to look back at the busted up harvester lying crippled on the deck. "And maybe a bit of smoke inhalation," he added with a cough, "but otherwise we're good. Thanks for waiting for us."

*"No problem, Captain. And welcome back."*

"Thanks. We'll see you shortly."

*"Copy,"* Cameron answered, before adding, *"And tell Josh he's got a date."*

Nathan smiled as he watched Josh and his copilot Loki slide down off the top of the harvester and onto the deck. They had been forced to climb out through emergency escape hatches directly above their seats, since the twisted wreckage made it impossible for them to pass through into the back cabin from the cockpit. As they walked toward him, Josh, who until this moment had always been covered up by helmet and faceplate, removed his helmet revealing a mound of shaggy blond hair atop a boyish face that looked to be maybe eighteen years old at best. He was small and wiry and looked like he was wearing his older brother's flight suit as he flashed a ragged smile and extended his hand to Nathan.

"I'll tell him," Nathan laughed as he clicked off his mic. "Nice flying, mister," Nathan said, shaking Josh's hand.

"Thank you, Captain," Josh answered, eagerly soaking up the praise.

"You, my friend, can call me Nathan."

"Josh," he returned, "and this is my copilot, Loki."

"Pleasure, sir," the slightly older copilot greeted as he shook Nathan's hand.

"Where'd you guys learn to fly like that?" Nathan asked.

Josh smiled. "VR games. Where else?"

Nathan laughed. "Where else, indeed." Nathan turned to look toward Tug's ship as Josh and Loki headed into the hangar bay. Tug was already down on the deck, hugging his girls, with Jalea standing nearby. Vladimir was catching Jessica as she slid down off the fighter, giving her his customary bear hug of a greeting. Nathan headed over to them. "You saved our ass," Nathan told her as he neared.

"Hell, Tug did all the work. I was just along for the ride."

Nathan wrapped his arms around her, feeling more affection for her at that moment than he expected. "We thought we'd lost you," he whispered as he hugged her.

"I'm kind of hard to kill," she bragged.

"Yeah, I'm starting to realize that," Nathan agreed as he pulled away. "Come on. Let's go see how much Cam has banged up the ship while we were gone."

"Oh Bozhe," Vladimir declared, realizing he probably had a host of new problems to repair after the pounding the ship had just taken. "Please, do not say this."

Nathan stepped over to Tug, who still had his arms around his daughters. "Thanks, Tug. You saved our butts."

"Respectfully, Captain," Tug began as he shook Nathan's hand, "it was not you I was trying to save," he added, his gaze returning to his girls.

"Jalea," Nathan called as they headed toward the hangar bay, "will you escort Tug and his family to medical?"

\* \* \*

"Captain on the bridge!" the marine at the doorway announced as Nathan entered, appearing more confident than ever before.

"Report, Commander."

"We're down to eight rail gun turrets, and we had a few more chunks taken out of our hull. But as we took them head on, main propulsion and power are both fully operational, as is the jump drive."

"I'll bet our underside isn't pretty. Nice move, by the way."

"Thanks."

"Where are we?"

"Thirty-eight light minutes from Haven, on a course headed out of the system at quarter light. As best we can tell, the enemy ship has not yet detected our new position. Theoretically, it should take at least another twenty minutes before we will appear on their sensors."

"But we can't be sure of that," Nathan pointed out.

"Sir?" Cameron asked, a bit confused.

"We don't really know their sensor capabilities."

"But the speed of light is constant, regardless..."

"Yes, of course. But let's just assume that they have much better detection capabilities. Better to err on the side of caution at this point."

Cameron was shocked. It was the first time she had ever seen Nathan take the *safe* route. "Yes, sir."

"Abby, how soon can we jump again?"

"We're at ninety percent capacity, Captain. And I already have a jump plotted that would take us back to the point where we originally entered this system. We can jump at any time, up to nine light years if necessary."

"Very well."

"Captain," Jessica interrupted, "the Ta'Akar are obviously actively pursuing us. If Tug's right about this Caius guy…"

"Ready room, Jess," Nathan ordered, pointing toward the back of the bridge. "Cam, join us."

Jessica immediately realized that although she had been relatively free to disagree with Nathan on Haven, on board, decorum dictated otherwise.

"Who's Caius?" Cameron asked as she followed Nathan and Jessica into the captain's ready room. "And who are the Ta'Akar, for that matter?"

"The Takarans," Nathan told her. "Apparently we were mispronouncing their name."

"And Caius?"

"I'm pretty sure he's some kind of leader—a dictator, or a king, maybe," Jessica explained. "If what Tug was saying is true, then the Ta'Akar will stop at nothing to find us and capture our jump drive."

"Who is Tug?" Cameron asked, feeling more and more out of the loop with each passing moment.

"The farmer we bought the molo from," Nathan answered.

"I'm pretty sure he's more than a farmer," Jessica added.

"Apparently he was a fighter pilot at some point," Nathan explained to Cameron as he sat down. "Damaged in battle, drifted, ended up stranded on Haven and became a farmer."

"Oh, I think there's more to him than he's lettin' on," Jessica insisted. "I was in his kitchen, just after they captured him and killed his wife."

"What?" Cameron was getting more lost by the minute. "What the *hell* happened down there?"

Jessica continued, ignoring Cameron's remarks. "I heard them talking about how they would be decorated for capturing him alive. '*By Caius himself,*'" she explained. "Now tell me, how would the capture of a simple fighter jock warrant a personal commendation by their exalted leader?"

"You think he's somebody important?"

"I think he's at least somebody they want captured or killed, that's for damned sure. And that leads me to my next question," she added. "Was there a reason Tug was the guy we ended up doing business with?"

Nathan looked at her. The thought had crossed his mind more than once over the past few hours, but until now it was nothing more than an unsubstantiated suspicion. He reached over and hit his comm-button. "Comm, call medical. Have them send Jalea and Tug up here, ASAP."

"*Yes, sir.*"

"And send Abby in as well."

"*Yes, sir.*"

"What do you need Abby for?" Cameron wondered aloud.

"Tug told us something about a power source

that was being developed by the Ta'Akar. Something that could provide limitless power. He said they have nearly finished it."

Abby entered the ready room a moment later. "You asked to see me, Captain?"

"Yes, Doctor. Once before, you said that the range of the jump drive was only limited by the amount of power we were currently able to put into it. Is that true?"

"Theoretically, yes. If given enough power, as well as the ability to accurately calculate a long distance jump, you could jump between galaxies as easily as you would between stars. It would be a bit more difficult in practice, however. Why do you ask?"

"Theoretically, if we had access to a power source that was say, a hundred times more powerful than what we're currently using, would that help get us back to Earth any faster?"

"Yes, if it could be properly interfaced and calibrated to work with our systems, it might be of use."

"How much use?"

"You're asking me to make a lot of guesses, here, Captain."

"Indulge me, please."

"With a hundred times more power, we might be able to get back in a few jumps. Maybe even one."

"So, home in days or weeks instead of months, correct?"

"If everything went correctly, yes, it is possible." Abby looked at him for a moment. "Are you saying you have access to such a power source?"

"We have intelligence that suggests there may be something of this nature in existence out here," he admitted.

"Captain," Abby urged, "if we could find and utilize this power source, the advantage that the jump drive would provide the Earth would be increased exponentially."

"Yeah, that's what I was thinking," Nathan told her. "Thank you, Doctor. That's all for now."

Abby looked in each of their eyes as she turned to leave. There was obviously far more going on than she knew about. But the news of a potential power source gave her hope for the first time in a week—hope that she might still return to her husband and children once again.

"Nathan," Cameron started after Abby left, "that might explain why we came out with so little damage—and why they didn't fire any nukes this time."

"What are you talking about?"

"They wanted to capture us," Jessica interrupted, "to get our jump drive. They know about the jump drive."

"Then Tug was right," Nathan said, plopping down in his chair.


"You are sure they will be well cared for?" Tug was not happy about having to leave his daughters in the care of strangers, especially after having just lost their mother.

"They are good people," Jalea promised him.

"You have only known them for a handful of days, Jalea," he reminded her as they left medical en route to see the captain.

"Yet in that short time, we have been through much together." She noticed Tug looking back to medical as they left. "The doctor is well trained, and their injuries are minor."

"But their technology is primitive," he worried.

"Not all of it," she reminded him.

"Yes. This jump drive the captain spoke of, does it really work as he claims?"

"We are alive, are we not?"

"And you have *seen* it?"

"Several times now."

"It is difficult to believe," he said as they started up the ramp to the command deck.

They walked in silence for several moments before Tug spoke again. "Is this why you brought them to me?"

"I don't understand your meaning," Jalea lied.

"You forget; I know you only too well, Jalea. You have tried on more than one occasion to convince me to return to your cause."

Jalea stopped walking and turned to him, angered by his comments. "It isn't my cause; it's our cause," she said, trying to control her temper, glancing back and forth to make sure nobody could hear them. "And it once was *your* cause, or have you already forgotten?"

"I have forgotten *nothing*," he snapped back, his own anger at her insolence bubbling to the surface. "I was fighting the Ta'Akar while you were still suckling at your mother's bosom!" he reminded her under his breath. "Do not behave as if you are the only one of us that has suffered great loss. I too have suffered, more than you can possibly imagine." Tug stopped and calmed himself before continuing. "Do not try and manipulate me as you do others, Jalea. You may not care for my reaction," he added as he continued toward the bridge.

Tug took a few steps before he realized Jalea had

not moved. He turned back to face her, knowing that she had more to say.

"Thousands have died," Jalea began. "Two generations have suffered. And now, when we are scattered to the winds and all but defeated, the instrument of our salvation is delivered unto us. And you say you have had enough?" Jalea moved closer to Tug as she continued. "If we give up now, when victory is finally within our grasp, those that have fallen will have done so in vain. You would steal the meaning from their sacrifice? If we do this, how will we be judged by our maker?"

"I am certain we will all be judged harshly for our transgressions, dear Jalea. Of this I have no doubt."

Jalea moved even closer to Tug, placing her hands on his chest in a more intimate fashion as she gazed into his eyes. "And what of your daughters? What kind of life will they have under complete and utter domination by the Ta'Akar?"

Tug looked into Jalea's exotic green eyes, remembering all that they had once been to each other. But that had been another life, another time. He placed his hands on top of hers. "You can turn off your charms, Jalea," he told her as he pulled her hands off his chest and dropped them at her sides. "I will not allow my daughters to be crushed under the heel of Caius."

Tug turned and resumed his journey to the bridge. Jalea smiled wryly and followed. He might no longer take her to his bed, but he was still susceptible to her ways.

\* \* \*

"Thank you for coming," Nathan said as Jalea

and Tug entered the room. "I trust your daughters are okay?"

"Their injuries are minor. Thank you."

"I am truly sorry about your wife."

"Thank you, Captain," Tug responded.

"Tug, this is my executive officer, Commander Taylor," Nathan introduced. "Commander, this is Redmon Tugwell."

Cameron stepped forward and shook Tug's hand. "A pleasure, sir. Thank you for aiding in the rescue of our people. And may I also express my condolences for your loss."

"Thank you, Commander." Tug turned back to Nathan. "You wished to speak with us?"

"Yes. Please, have a seat."

Tug and Jalea took the seats across the desk from Nathan, while Cameron and Jessica took seats on the couch.

"We seem to be at a crossroads of sorts," Nathan began as he retook his seat. "And before we can decide which path to take, we need to clear up a few things. I was hoping that you might be able to help us in this regard."

"I will do what I can, Captain."

Nathan looked at Jalea. As usual, she showed no indication of her emotional state. Tug, on the other hand, showed far more in his expressions and mannerisms. The question was whether or not they were genuine.

"Last night, I was quite forthcoming in my detailing of our current situation as well as our immediate goals. And I felt, at the time, that you had been just as forthcoming."

Tug got the hidden meaning in Nathan's carefully chosen words. "And now you have reason to suspect otherwise?"

Nathan wasn't sure how the next step was going to play out. He had an advantage at the moment that he felt compelled to press. Tug and his daughters were literally at his mercy. As distasteful as playing that advantage was to him, he felt he had little choice. Under different circumstances, he would probably not choose this course of action. Now, however, the stakes were too high.

"Yes, I'm afraid I do," Nathan admitted. "While my security chief was covertly preparing to rescue you, she overheard a conversation between your captors. They were anticipating considerable favor for your capture, possibly even decoration by some of your highest leaders." Nathan let that hang for a moment, looking for a reaction in either of their faces. As suspected, none were of use.

"The over-excitement of inexperienced soldiers," Tug offered, "perhaps combined with a case of mistaken identity."

"Uh-huh." Nathan glanced over at Jessica. She wasn't buying it any more than he was. "I don't think so," he disagreed. "You see, I noticed a few other things as well. Like, why our attackers seemed unconcerned with our capture, choosing instead to attack everyone with deadly force." Nathan noticed a brief, sidelong glance from Tug to Jalea, one to which Jalea offered no reaction. "Or why that warship didn't blast us to pieces with nukes. Now why is that?"

"I cannot speak of the motivations of others, Captain, but I see no value in the capture of a farmer to the Ta'Akar."

Nathan was surprised that Tug was still trying to hide the truth from him. It angered him that either one or both of them were trying to play him for a fool at the risk of his life, the well being of his ship and crew, and quite possibly of his entire world.

Nathan leaned back in his chair, letting out a long, slow breath as he did so. He looked over at Jessica and then Cameron. Neither of them gave any indication of what they were thinking.

Nathan nodded at Jessica, who pressed a button on her data pad. Tug's recorded voice came from the device. *"I have shed as much blood as any man could and still live to tell. This last battle was nearly my undoing. My wounds are still not yet fully healed."* Jessica pressed another button to fast-forward to the next clip. *"My days as a Karuzari are over, Jalea. It is time for another to pick up the flag in my place."*

Tug stared at Nathan for a moment, anger and betrayal in his eyes. "You are more resourceful than I gave you credit for, Captain."

Nathan was tired. He was tired of the stress. He was tired of the responsibility, and more importantly, he was tired of the games. But he was also tired of looking to others to make decisions for him. He had done that his entire life, not really caring enough to make up his own mind. That had started to change when he joined the fleet. That had been the beginning of a real change in his life. And what had started out as a way to get away from everything for a few years and start over had somehow turned into a test of fate—his own, his crew's, and even his world's.

Nathan looked at Cameron and Jessica again, as he said, "Let's cut the bullshit, shall we?" Cameron's eyes widened. Jessica smiled slightly, waiting to see where Nathan was going. "You want to know what I think? I think one or both of you cooked all this up to suck us into your little rebellion." Nathan suddenly leaned forward again. "At first, I thought you were looking for a way to hijack my ship," he said to Jalea. "Then you started in with all that *'gift from God'* crap the other day. Now I think you're trying to make us an ally."

"Is it working?" There was no emotion in Jalea's question, and no expression on her face when the question was asked.

"Kind of, yeah," he admitted.

Cameron leaned in to Jessica, whispering, "What the hell is he doing?"

"I have no idea," Jessica whispered back, "but this should be good."

"But not for the same reasons as you," Nathan continued. "I've got one goal and one goal only—to get my ship and our jump drive back to Earth, before it's too late. Now as long as our individual goals are mutually beneficial, I'm willing to play along. But there are conditions."

"Such as?" Jalea asked.

"Such as, who the hell are you, Tug? And why do the Ta'Akar want you so badly?"

Tug sighed. "Because I was the leader of the Karuzari."

"Whoa," Jessica muttered under her breath.

For the first time since they entered the room, Nathan thought he saw a reaction of some sort on Jalea's face. She wasn't happy with his revelation.

"That would explain a lot," Nathan said.

"Yeah, it would," Jessica agreed, "like the shield, for starters."

Nathan looked a little skeptical. "Isn't Haven kind of far away from the action?"

"It did present logistical difficulties, but it was a

necessary precaution."

"And the power source you spoke of? Does it really exist, or was that just a ruse to gain our allegiance?"

"I assure you, Captain, the device is real, as is the threat posed by its completion. In this I have been completely truthful. This is why I continued to lead the Karuzari for as long as I did, despite the objections of my late wife."

Nathan noticed Tug's steely gaze becoming more intense as he spoke.

"I fought the Ta'Akar for more than twenty years," Tug continued. "Ranni is the third love I have lost because of the Ta'Akar—because of Caius. When I came to Haven, in much the way I described, I left that life behind me. But sometimes fate does not let go so easily. Sometimes it finds you, no matter how hard you try to hide from its cold embrace." Tug took a deep breath, steadying himself. "It seems that fate once again has me in its clutches, Captain, as I believe it now has you. So the question, Captain, is will we face our fates together?"

Nathan looked at Jalea. Her big green eyes, as seductive as ever, beckoned him. He looked at Cameron. Her eyes showed grave concern. Jessica's, well hers seemed more entertained than anything. "It seems that fate has placed us on the same path, at least for now. I cannot promise you for how long we will travel this road together. But for the time being, you may consider us your ally."

"I am grateful for this, Captain," Tug said.

"We have much to discuss in the hours ahead," Nathan told him, "but for now, I have a ship to take care of, and you have daughters that require their father's attention."

Tug nodded agreement. "I am at your disposal, Captain." Tug rose from his seat and departed the ready room, with Jalea following him.

"Damn, Nathan!" Jessica exclaimed.

Nathan looked at Cameron. "Well?" he asked.

Cameron just shook her head, breathing in deeply. "I hope you know what you're doing, Nathan."

Nathan leaned back in his chair. "So do I."

20875876R00144

Printed in Great Britain
by Amazon